# RHYM

# USELESS

# Rhymes with Useless

### Stories by

### Terence Young

*Raincoast Books acknowledges the ongoing support of The Canada Council; the British Columbia Ministry of Small Business, Tourism and Culture through the BC Arts Council; and the Government of Canada through the Book Publishing Industry Development Program (BPIDP).*

First published in 2000 by

Raincoast Books
9050 Shaughnessy Street
Vancouver, B.C.
V6P 6E5
(604) 323-7100

www.raincoast.com

Edited by Joy Gugeler
Typeset by Bruce Collins
Cover photo by Les Smith
Cover design by Les Smith

1 2 3 4 5 6 7 8 9 10

CANADIAN CATALOGUING IN PUBLICATION DATA

Young, Terence.
  Rhymes with useless

ISBN 1-55192-354-8

  I. Title.
PS8597.O72R59 2000      C813'.54      C00-910711-8
PR9199.3.Y69R59 2000

Printed and bound in Canada.

*To my mother,*
*to my sister Joan*
*and to the memory of my father*

# Contents

# RHYMES WITH
# USELESS

I did the math: two months without sex, pushing three. Meanwhile, Billie was saying that it didn't matter if Linda McCartney had been more tone-deaf than Yoko Ono, at least she'd had her head screwed on right.

"She wouldn't talk to meat eaters. Wouldn't even talk to them. If Linda found out you were eating meat, that was it. Game over. You were dead to her."

I shook my head. "Poor choice of words," I said.

"Go ahead and laugh — "

"I'm not laughing."

" — because the woman made sense. I understood her perfectly." Billie had her fingers splayed, ready to itemize the key points. "There are two types of people in this world. Those who eat meat and those that don't. It's that clear, Eustace. Don't let anybody tell you different. A meat eater is the kind of person who says it's okay to murder and exploit."

Billie, I and Hay Soo, our dog, were walking, shoulders into a salty southwestern whisper, the kind of breeze that blows nearly all the time down the strait from the open Pacific. We were ambling along one of Victoria's cliff-top paths that run above a pebbled shelf of beach. It's a popular place for joggers, dog people, kamikaze roller bladers, hang gliders and windsurfers. We were on the return leg of the circuit, just rounding the cairn at Holland point, when a woman passed us going the other way. She was in her early 20s — a girl really — toothsome, blonde. I turned to Billie.

"Did I ever tell you about the time Joni Mitchell cut my hair?"

"Get out of here," Billie said.

Billie discovered low-fat vegetarianism when her mother had a stroke just over 18 months ago. Seventy years of bacon grease and whipped cream had reduced her arteries to pinholes. When we visited her in the cardiac ward, she said she remembered seeing venetian blinds and then nothing at all. After the doctors had rooted out all the plaque and sludge, they stapled her shut and sent her home. Billie sat by her bedside and read to her. She read her John Robbins, the man who turned down an empire of ice cream to follow his high-fibre heart. She read her Dean Ornish. She read her Susan Powter. After two weeks of pinto beans and brown rice, her blood pressure dropped to 110 over 60. The GP was surprised, but skeptical. He asked her what diet she was on.

"It's no' a diet, laddie," she told him. "I'm Veegan. I'm bloody Veegan."

What was good for Billie's mother was good for us, too. No meat, no eggs, no dairy. No sex wasn't part of the plan. It just happened. These days we look forward to a nice baked potato with a splatter of homemade salsa.

"I am serious," I said, and I was. I was serious about changing the conversation. There was only so much I could take of Billie's endless fat facts, especially on the one day of decent weather we'd had in a month. Hay Soo was leading us around like a diesel locomotive. The trees beside the path were shaking. Everything was leafless. "Joni Mitchell cut my hair," I repeated.

"When?" Billie asked. "Last week?"

"No," I said.

Billie was being sarcastic, but I had to watch it. She's got a tongue that'll run you down the second you step off the curb. People used to shake their heads and say only a fool would marry Billie Pritchard. *Man of the moment*, she asked me once, *are you a fool?* This when all my mouth was good for was *Yes, oh yes, sweet thing, come on home.* Sometimes I really don't know. Billie said, "Maybe it was last summer while I was away. Maybe she cut it then. Hopped in her jet and scooted up from L.A. just because you were getting a little long on top."

Billie couldn't shake me. "Wrong again," I said. "This was before you and I met."

"Go ahead," she said. "I refuse to be shocked."

I used to think sex between Billie and me was not unlike two animals talking. Nice animals. Otters or polar bears. It was as easy as breathing. We never got winded. We never ran out of conversation. We jabbered on and did so anywhere we pleased. One Christmas we discovered the kitchen counter was the perfect height for a man my size. We grew fond of certain chairs over the years, some closets too. I remember telling Billie once that sex was a way to say everything without words, the silent confessional. She says I use sex as an excuse not to talk. She says I have no idea what real communication is. Billie has said this for as long as I have known her.

I wasn't in the mood for another one of Billie's rants — I already knew more about osteoporosis than can be good for any one person. The blonde girl who'd passed us earlier was bobbing around in my head like a plank in a river. It seemed only natural to grab on. So I said to Billie, "There was a man called Beverly and then there was Joni Mitchell. This was up north. I had gone there to look for work. The man's not really important, except that he almost killed someone, and Joni probably isn't important either, but she was nice enough to cut my hair."

"Eustace," Billie said.

I had her attention now. "Yes?" I said.

"What are you doing?"

"I'm talking," I said. "I am conveying a small part of my life's history, which I consider significant."

"That's what I thought," Billie said.

I stopped to tie my shoelace and passed the leash to Billie. A few of Hay Soo's dog friends were in the field beside us.

I put my hand in Billie's pocket. "Where was I?"

"You were saying you went north — "

" — to earn a living," I said, remembering my place. "Nothing could be truer."

"You never said where, precisely," Billie said, "but it doesn't matter. Names of towns mean nothing to me." And in fact they don't.

I painted a picture. "Let's say all the cars were angle-parked against the curb. Let's say there were houses on the main strip right beside bars and heavy-equipment retailers. Let's say that mountains hung around the place like thugs and that I booked myself into the Lakelse Hotel and slept for a whole day, right through to the maid knocking on the door. And then let's say I went out looking for work."

"Yes," said Billie. "Let's say all of that."

I went on. "There was a highway outfit working out of a storefront — Kewitt Construction — and an old man with a hardhat was sitting at the front desk. He told me about a survey crew leaving the next day for the Nass Valley. They still needed a rodman. I told him I'd like that, because I genuinely thought I would. He asked me my name. I said 'Eustace,' even spelled it out for him. I told him that it rhymed with 'useless' and that I didn't mind if he laughed. 'Everybody does the first time they hear it,' I said. He pointed to his hardhat, the letters *BEV* written across the front in black. He asked me if I knew what they were short for. 'Beverly?' I asked and he said 'Good guess.' I said, 'Oh,' and he said I could have the job except for one little thing."

"I already know about the hair," Billie said. "It gets cut off, doesn't it, Samson?"

"You know about the hair. But what do you know?"

"You were a victim of harsher times?"

"I was that," I said.

"You couldn't help yourself?"

"Precisely," I said.

"Well, then."

"Well, nothing. Beverly knew all that too. At least I thought he did. I told him the name of my hotel. He said that's where he was and that he'd bring around the payroll forms that evening for me to sign. I said 'Sure,' and he looked at me while I wrote down the room number. I felt sick. I walked out of the office and headed south along the main street. I stopped at a gas station. A girl was pumping gas."

Billie had her hand inside my pocket now. "Wait a minute," she said.

"All right," I said. We stopped walking.

"It wasn't her," she said. She took her hand back. I could see she wanted to list a few points.

"Whoever do you mean?" I asked.

"The girl at the gas station," Billie said. "You're not about to tell me you stumbled on Joni Mitchell killing time as a pump jockey. Not the Joni Mitchell who sang at Woodstock. You can't expect me to buy a lie as dumb as that."

"She said she was." I lifted my shoulders into an apologetic shrug.

Billie rolled her eyes. "And you believed her?"

"You didn't hear her sing," I said.

"Really."

"There's an amazing echo in most gas stations. All that cement."

"What did she look like?" Billie asked.

"Blonde, thin."

"So was I, once."

"I remember."

I told Billie I walked back and forth in front of that station with the scum of an idea lingering on my tongue. I told her how the highway was powdered with summer dust and how Joni was running from pump to pump, filling the downtime with talk, using her hands as if she were a cheerleader, pointing down the highway, up at the mountains. I told Billie she was *on*, lit up like a runway and waiting for the world to land.

"Cars came and went. Big trucks rolled by heavy with logs. I walked over to the front door. Joni was under a truck in one of the bays, a grease gun in her hand while she worked at the universals. She was singing — high, swooping lyrics that were nothing to me at the time. 'Can I use the phone?' I asked. She turned and said, 'Leave a dime on the counter' and went back to her song. I remember I yelled 'Thanks,' and then, because I didn't know any other way of saying what I wanted, I asked really quickly, 'Will you cut my hair?' To hear me, you might've thought I was asking her to top up the oil and check the tires. The thing is, I don't remember Joni putting up a fuss or staring at me like I had two heads. I suppose that I must have explained about the job and that I hated the idea of going to one of the local barbers. Whatever I told her must have sounded convincing, because she said 'Yes' and told me to come back after her shift."

⌗

We were nearing the end of the ocean path. Houses were coming into view beyond a fringe of trees. "Now I'm jealous," Billie said.

"How do you mean?" I asked. I was scanning ahead for Hay Soo. He'd slipped from his collar a few minutes earlier.

"I'm jealous of anybody in love," she said.

I had anticipated this reaction. "This wasn't love," I said. "All she did was cut my hair."

"Not with *her*, sweetheart," Billie said. "You were in love with yourself."

"Right," I said. I've always told Billie she should take up archery, with an aim like hers.

Billie said once she would never go out of her way to straighten me out, or any man, for that matter. "There's no real fun in something so obvious," she'd said, "and besides, it would be a full-time job." In the news a couple of weeks back, there was a story about a sex-change operation. In the "Living" section. When Billie finished reading about how Mark/Marjory had never been happier, she said she wasn't one bit surprised.

"I'd lop mine off too, if I had one," she said.

I pointed out to her that there had also been moves in the other direction.

"I've never said there aren't stupid women," she said.

Billie says she wouldn't be a man for all the money in the world. "Too much pressure," she says. "Anybody with a good set of lungs can shout that thing back down and then what good is it? Look at you, Eustace. You've been worrying yourself to death for months and over what? A fingerful of flesh that wouldn't even keep a bird alive."

Sometimes I think the switch to low fat killed my sex drive. My body was used to eggs in the morning, a slice of buttered bread. Not lentils. Not bulgar. Not whole-wheat tortillas. Most of me still believes in all that protein swimming around in my glands, lighting the big fuse. Billie says I'm a classic food victim. She says I was lucky any blood got to my dick at all the way I kept packing on the cholesterol. I've bought books on Tantric yoga. My chakras are in good shape. I went to Chinatown and bought 30 glass vials of royal jelly mixed with ginseng. I took two a day until they ran out. I bought more. Lately I'm thinking bear liver, rhinoceros horn. It's not that sex is the only thing on my mind. Billie tells me to relax. She says she could have an orgasm with my elbow if she wanted. The way I see it, I'm far too relaxed as it is, if you know what I mean.

"Maybe you'd better tell me about the hotel now," Billie said. There was a burr in her voice, a kind of surliness.

"What do you need to know?" I asked. Anybody who takes the wheel with Billie along should have some idea where he is going.

"What was the lake like, for instance?" Billie asked.

"Lake?"

"Lakelse," she said. "You said it was the Lakelse Hotel."

"I don't remember there being any lake," I said. "There were some hot springs outside town, but I never went there."

"So, no lake," Billy said.

"No," I said. I caught a glimpse of Hay Soo. He and a Lab cross were making out next to a park bench.

"Anything remarkable about the hotel?" she asked. "This Lakelse Hotel. What kind of a name is that, anyway? There's no lake, you said. So is it something 'else'?"

"Don't ask me. All I remember is there was a country lounge in the basement."

"Is that where you waited?"

"What do you mean?" I asked.

"For your rendezvous with Joni at the gas station," she said.

"Not me," I said. "I waited in my room."

"Proceed then," Billie said. "I'm tired of guessing now."

"Yes, all right," I said and I told her what happened next.

‡

"I walked back to the hotel but started feeling sorry for myself. I watched TV until there was a knock on my door. Beverly came by with the papers and a bottle. He was already stinking when I let him in. 'Happy days,' he said to me, holding up the bottle. Anybody will tell you there isn't much space to park another body in one of those rooms, but he pulled up a chair close to the bed and unwrapped two glasses from the bedside table before I could think of anything to say. He poured a couple of fingers in each. Then he waved me over. 'Drink up,' he said. The glass was half full of rye. He tilted his glass back. I sipped mine. There was grease on his hair that smelled bad.

"He was quiet a minute. Then he said, 'I'm a little drunk.'

"'I thought so,' I said.

"'Oh,' he said. 'Is this your first job?'

"'I've worked before.'

"'I don't doubt it.'

"'But this is different,' I said.

"'It will be,' Beverly said.

"'That's good.'

"'I'm glad to hear you say that.'

"I didn't say anything. He topped up my glass.

"'You'll see what I mean when you head up to camp tomorrow. Those kids are all along the river. They lie in the sun and sometimes hold up traffic.'

"He was starting to scare me. 'Yes,' I said. 'I guess I'll see.'

"'You bet your white ass you will,' Beverly said.

"He got up to use the toilet and while he was gone I looked over the papers. One was a tax form that asked me my marital status. There was another that listed all the payroll deductions I had to agree to. Beverly came back into the room, only now he had his shirt off. He was holding it over his arm. He sat down beside me on the bed.

"'Do me a favour, kid?' he asked. 'I'm all fingers and thumbs,' he said and shoved the shirt into my lap.

"'I guess that can be a problem,' I said, but I didn't pick up the shirt. I was calculating the distance between the bed and the door, deciding whether I could take the old guy if things turned ugly. Beverly reached into his pocket and pulled out a box.

"'There's one missing on the cuff and another on the collar,' he said. He opened the box to reveal a needle and thread, a few buttons in a pill bottle.

"'Okay,' I said. My hands were shaking when I picked up the box. I looked at everything. The thread. The shirt. The bottle.

Cheap Canadian rye was burning a hole in my stomach. I worried I might throw up. Some distant part of me recognized what was going on, was even trying to tell me to get up and leave, but another part of me was shrugging its shoulders. 'You can do this,' it said.

"I had never really sewn anything before, but the buttons stayed on. I signed the papers and Beverly left. I fell asleep until it was time to go and have my hair cut. I walked out of the hotel into the full light of day. It was nearly nine o'clock, but it looked like the sun wasn't ever going to set. Joni was waiting for me with a pair of scissors and a brush. When I calmed down, she told me her name. She spelled it with a *y* back then. I asked only because it was my sister's name, too. She ends hers with *ie*. Joni said she wanted to go to industrial arts school. She liked music, but she really wanted to weld things. I told her some guy had just asked me to sew his shirt for him. She laughed. Any fool could tell she was born to sing. I was sitting on a stack of used tires behind the station with the northern sun in my eyes. I said maybe it was about time I got my hair cut, if people were bringing me their clothes to fix. She said I had beautiful hair. It was a shame to cut it, she said. Joni did a good job. I paid her $10. She wanted the hair too, so I gave it to her."

We turned onto our street. Hay Soo's breath was steaming. The weather was turning colder. Billie was quiet. I knew she was adding things up, reviewing the critical details. Before long she spoke. She said, "You fixed the man's shirt and Joni cut your hair."

"Yes," I said.

"Maybe she still has it."

"What's that?" I asked, but I knew what she meant.

"Your hair," Billie said.

"I doubt it," I said.

"That's not the whole story, is it, Eustace?"

"No," I said.

"I was ready to leave at eight the next morning, but nobody showed up 'til ten. Even then it wasn't the survey crew. It was only Beverly and he didn't say much except 'Get in.' I found out later he'd spent the night drinking and had forgotten to tell the crew about me. There wasn't much he could do except drive me to the camp himself. He didn't say anything about my hair. He didn't say much at all. I would like to say he whistled, but it was really a sound he made with his teeth by blowing through a gap. It was only one note, but he kept it going as long as he could.

"We drove out of town, past the gas station where Joni worked, but she wasn't there. I remembered her telling me she had the day off. We drove over the bridge and up the river road. It was a hot July day. Dust came in through the floorboards. Beverly put the fan on high to blow it back out. I had my window all the way down. School was out. All along the roadside there were pickups parked facing the river with speakers on their roofs. Kids were lying on the shoulder, down the bank, on big boulders in the current. Some had even spread their towels on the road and were lying in the sun. They were smoking cigarettes and dope, too. A few longhairs floated among the cars. I spotted Joni playing guitar and singing to a small crowd under a tree. Once in a while, someone would yell something at the truck or slap a fender as we went by. Beverly didn't once speed up, but his foot was heavy on the gas. It was quite likely he hated those kids. He just looked straight ahead and whistled.

"We rounded a turn and in the middle of the road was a kid in a swimsuit lying facedown on a towel sunning himself. There was room to go around him, so I wasn't worried. But we drove over his legs. Not fast. Just one bump and then another. I looked through the rear window. It was only a little Ford Courier, but still. Beverly stopped whistling and turned to me. He was smiling. All he said was, 'We killed better than that in World War Two.' Then he started whistling again."

⌗

"You just kept going?" Billie asked.

"Yes," I said. "All the way to camp."

"Was the kid hurt?" asked Billie.

"Chances were in his favour," I told her. "It was only a compact."

Billie was quiet a minute. We sidestepped a couple with a pair of binoculars. Two bald eagles were sitting on a branch near the top of a dead cottonwood. The tree was shining like old bones, the bark long gone. Hay Soo couldn't care less about the birds, he was so tired.

"You figure Joni recognized you?" she asked. "She was there, you said. You said she was down by the river with her guitar, so it stands to reason she might've."

"Can't say," I said.

"Even if she didn't," Billie said.

"Yes," I said. "Even if she didn't."

We were nearly home. Billie and I were now dragging the dog. I opened the gate and hauled Hay Soo onto the sundeck, where he flopped down under the picnic table. When I turned around, Billie was leaning against the front door wagging her finger at me.

"What?" I said.

"Come inside," she said.

"You want to hear more?" I asked. Skin started to tighten

around my neck. "I cut my hair because some drunk told me to. I did nothing while he drove over a kid's legs. I compromised the few ideals I ever had and you want more? There is no more."

"Oh, I liked all that stuff," she said. "The hair. The truck. The boy on the road. I liked everything but those buttons."

Something thick and heavy was crawling up the back of my throat. I watched Billie turn around and head toward the stairs.

"Show me, Eustace," I heard her say from somewhere inside. "You show me exactly how you did it."

# FAST

Jerry told Sarah to look at it as a couples thing, an evening with the neighbours, a Welcome Wagon, glad-you-moved-in, hope-you-feel-at-home, let's-drink-a-little-wine kind of thing. But Sarah and Jerry were meeting an investment counsellor.

They were living in the city then and had just rented the upper two floors of a house on the east side near the Italian coffee merchants and the Vietnamese fruit and vegetable vendors. Each day they took the bus up 10th to the university, where they'd been working for the past few months. Sarah was in awards and loans and Jerry serviced photocopy machines. They sat in on lectures, sometimes went to readings. It was like being students again without the course work. Campus daycare was the best in the city. Things couldn't have been better.

It was Sarah who answered the call from the neighbours. Jerry had gone to the market to pick up a few things: a box of beer, a jar of peanuts, diapers. When he got back, she told him Mrs. Underwood had asked them over for dinner.

"She said she wants to break the ice," Sarah said. Anna hung in the doorway, her feet pounding the linoleum under the Jolly Jumper. She was too big for the contraption, but it kept her happy.

"What ice?" Jerry asked. "We met them on moving day. They watched, we worked, everybody talked. Ice all gone." He threw a peanut at Anna.

"It's a little more than dinner, Jerry," Sarah said.

"Call me Art," Jerry said. He'd poured a handful of salted peanuts from the jar and was throwing them at Anna, who bounced higher and higher with each peanut.

"What?" Sarah asked.

"The husband. I asked him what his name was and he said, 'Call me Art.'"

"Stop doing that, you moron. Anna's not a monkey." Sarah began to pick peanuts up off the floor.

"Yes, she is. She's a little monkey, aren't you, Anna? Daddy's little monkey."

"You're the only ape in this house, Jerry," Sarah said. She took the jar of peanuts, put it in a kitchen cupboard and closed the door with a bang. Like an echo, the door to the basement suite slammed shut beneath them and moments later a car's engine wound up to a crescendo and then faded into the distance.

"So what's her name?" Jerry asked. He got up to look out the window at the disappearing car.

"Who?"

"Mrs. Call me Art," Jerry said.

"Her name is Helen. The husband's a mutual funds dealer and she says he has a few ideas we might be interested in."

"They're Muslims, you know," Jerry said.

"Helen is not a Muslim," Sarah said. She picked up a facecloth and rinsed it with warm water.

"Not her. The people downstairs. The wife wears headgear," Jerry said. "There really is something sexy about a hidden face."

"Don't get any ideas," Sarah said. She washed Anna's hands,

kissed her and lifted her out of the Jolly Jumper. "I'm not your slave."

"Yes, but we could *pretend*," Jerry said. "After Anna's in bed. You could wrap yourself in a tablecloth."

"Dinner's Saturday, big boy," Sarah said.

Jerry had no training. Most of what he knew about copiers he'd picked up as a student. Whenever a department's machine jammed or ran out of dry ink, Jerry was called in. He replaced staples, programmed student user cards, even did a little repair work if the job wasn't serious. The heavy stuff he left for company reps. Things got ugly when he couldn't fix a simple problem. People hovered over him while he pulled out rollers and flicked dust from sensors. They looked at their watches and rolled their eyes when other people came into the room, sheaves of papers in their hands. They talked about him in the third person. *He's working on it*, they said to someone passing by for the fifth time. *He thinks it's a belt*, one person whispered above Jerry's head. They feared a total breakdown. Jerry thought it was disgusting the way professors flooded their students with handouts.

"Lazy bastards," he complained to Sarah. "They're scared they might actually have to do some real teaching."

He disliked the students too. Girls treated him like a construction worker, only one up the food chain from a rapist. Some walked around him as though he were diseased, others as though he didn't exist. None of them spoke to him. Their boyfriends looked past him, far down the hall, as though they were concentrating on their futures, on the years of hard work and success that lay ahead of them. *They'd* never be just some guy who ate his sandwich in the copy room sitting on an overturned recycle box.

"Those kids are too preoccupied with their own lives to think about yours," Sarah told him. "Don't be so paranoid." She asked him to remember what it was like when he was a student himself. Did he think less of people just because they worked in jobs like his? Jerry said he couldn't remember.

But he *was* pretty much his own man. Although they'd given him a pager, people rarely called. Some days he spent a few hours in the stacks, flipping through periodicals. There were certain secretaries he could flirt with too. A few even younger than Sarah. He'd ask to use the phone and then, while he was on hold to Xerox or Canon, he'd talk to them about their weekends, find out if they had kids. Pretty harmless, most of it. But he sensed it was more than just chat for some of them. There was that temp with long black hair, thick and full of curls, the kind of hair Jerry imagined gypsy women might have. She was always putting her hand on his arm when she was speaking to him, the way some people do to make a point, but she left it there longer than she needed to. When he asked her for something — paper to test a copier that was running low, say — she didn't hand it to him right away but kept it tucked against her chest until he actually had to look her in the eyes and ask for it again. He imagined going for coffee with her, or maybe a beer, just to talk to someone different. That didn't seem so bad.

One night he had a delicious dream. He was in a large old house, a Victorian brothel. Naked women walked in and out of various rooms, but instead of sex they offered him food, spicy meats and vegetable stews. They wanted him to lie down and open his mouth. They stood waiting with spoons in their hands. Jerry reached out for one of the women and the movement woke him up. But he could still smell the food. At first he thought he'd left something in the oven, maybe a pot on the stove, but when he got up to check, the oven was off and the elements were cold. He looked at the kitchen clock: 2:30 a.m.

"What's that smell?" Sarah asked him when he came back to the bedroom.

"It must be the people downstairs," Jerry said. He got down on the floor and pressed his ears to the carpet. Sarah joined him. Up through the joists came the sounds of pots clanging, an oven door opening and closing, taps running. They went to one of the hot-air vents and breathed in: bread, unmistakably, and a roast, the heavy scent of cumin.

"What are they doing down there?" Sarah asked.

"Eating," Jerry said.

"I don't think I can sleep with all that food cooking," Sarah said.

"So don't sleep," Jerry said, still aroused from his dream.

"You are such a pervert," Sarah said.

The next night the same thing happened. They went to bed and woke up around two or three, lured out of their sleep by the aromas seeping into their apartment from below. By the third night, Jerry found he was growing fond of the routine. As long as he'd eaten well himself, the smells didn't bother him, besides, he liked the idea of all that industry beneath him. Making love seemed more erotic too, perhaps because of his dream, but also because of the sensuous wave of spices. Anna started sleeping through the night and she seemed happier the next day, more willing to leave her parents at the daycare door and join in with the other children.

⌗

In the office of one of the university residences where Jerry serviced a coin-operated copier, he saw a sign addressed to all

Muslim students regarding cafeteria rebates during the month of Ramadan. One of the staff explained that Muslims fasted from sunrise to sunset during the ninth month of their calendar.

"But they can eat in between?" he asked.

"Yes," she said, "but we can't stay open just for them."

"You're not Muslim, are you?" Jerry asked.

"Christ, no," the woman said. "Do I look like one?"

"Just asking," Jerry said and then he went to the library.

⌗

"And they all do this?" Sarah asked Jerry when he told her later.

"All except pregnant women, the insane and people suffering from terminal or life-threatening diseases," Jerry recited from memory. "There are a few other exceptions, like prepubescent children, but otherwise everybody."

"How come I've never heard of it before?"

"How many Muslims do you know?" Jerry asked.

They sat together on the couch while Anna pulled tissues from a box of Kleenex. It was cheap entertainment and they loved to watch her.

"What's the point?" Sarah asked.

"What's the point of any religion?"

"No," Sarah said. "I mean the spiritual point. Is it humility? Purity?"

"Millions of people," Jerry said, "starving themselves while we're sitting here and then getting up in the middle of the night and eating like crazy? That's not humility. That's nuts."

"Do you think our Muslims share the cooking?" Sarah wanted to know. "Do you think they have an equitable, Western relationship?"

"I've only ever seen the back of her head, Sarah."

"Let's say they do."

"I could never make myself get up that early," Jerry said. "And who wants to look at a pot roast at two in the morning?"

"If you believed what they believe, you'd do it," Sarah said.

Anna had discovered a second box of Kleenex. Jerry thought about Saturday and their dinner with the Underwoods. Their lives were changing. They used to visit friends. Now they visited couples. Lately it was couples with kids and now they were having dinner with money managers.

Once, when another "adventure playground" seemed more than he could bear, they had taken Anna to a cemetery by the sea. Jerry had found a dead Sarah and then a dead Jerry. They'd taken pictures of each other beside their namesakes. They'd taken pictures of Anna peeking out from behind a broken headstone, grey November waves breaking behind her.

Children at the daycare invited Anna to birthday parties. Birthday parties meant presents and videos and return invitations. Return invitations meant party favours and goody bags and more videos. Jerry felt silly at first. He felt that he and Sarah were playing house. Now he didn't feel silly at all; he felt he was slipping away.

"I wish we had something we could do together like that," Sarah said. "It sounds romantic. The two of them down there in the middle of the night, helping each other stay faithful to God."

"Allah," Jerry said.

"Don't you think it's inspiring?" Sarah asked.

"I'll bet they cheat," Jerry said.

"Cheat?"

"Sneak a sandwich," Jerry said. "A bag of chips."

"Never."

It was getting dark. Kleenex tissues covered the floor in front of them. Jerry got up and waded over to Anna. He plucked her from the mess and held her high over his head.

"What *is* a mutual fund, Anna?" he asked. Anna spit a long thread of drool onto his nose.

"That's your first question Saturday night," Sarah said.

Helen Underwood cleared away the dessert dishes. An inverted flying saucer hung above the dining room table, its halogen bulb dimmed to complement the candles still burning after two hours. Jerry and Sarah's bottle of Chilean red, freshly uncorked, sat on the buffet. Sarah had moved her chair to face Arthur, who was explaining the benefits of dollar-cost averaging. Jerry tried to listen, sipping frequently from his glass.

"The idea is to think long term," Arthur was saying. "This is not some get-rich-quick scheme." He pointed at two contradictory lines on a graph.

"But still . . . ," Sarah said.

"Exactly," Arthur said. "You end up miles ahead of any savings account."

They'd arrived shortly before eight, Anna ready for bed, dressed in her pyjamas, teddies and bottles tucked into her night bag. The Underwoods had insisted they bring her. They kept toys around for occasions just like this, leftovers from the days their own children were young. "After all," Helen had said, "this is really about *her*, isn't it?" Jerry and Sarah had agreed.

They'd spent some time walking through the house, talking about the neighbourhood, the schools. There was a Montessori only a block away, great for artistic children. The Underwoods collected art. Paintings hung everywhere, local work, not because it was an investment — although nobody could dispute the returns — but because they liked it. They liked art, they liked helping young people, they liked children. It was as simple as that.

Arthur was liberal with the liquor, too. They'd had sherries before dinner, two bottles of wine during the meal. He'd been careful to fill their glasses whenever the wine fell below half. Sarah had asked for soda water after a while, but Jerry had kept drinking. At one point, he'd asked where Anna was. Sarah had given him a dirty look. She had told him he'd put her to sleep in the Underwoods' bedroom. Didn't he remember how he'd lain down on the floor beside her and drifted off himself? Didn't he remember her coming and getting him? Jerry had slapped his forehead as though he'd just locked his keys in his car. He'd covered his glass with his hand and made the sign of the cross. Arthur had laughed and filled the glass anyway.

"Self-directed if you want," Arthur said, "though I wouldn't recommend it at first. The thing you want to do is leverage and let it build for a while. Then you can start shuffling things around."

Earlier that afternoon, Sarah had told Jerry to have an open mind. They'd gone to the dog park so Anna could watch the owners throw Frisbees and tennis balls to their pets. Anna liked to pet the smaller dogs, got excited when her favourites showed up. A stand of poplars divided the park from a busy avenue and there was a community vegetable garden. Couples had been busy turning over soil, raking up dead leaves and weeds. Sarah and Jerry had walked the perimeter of the park.

Money was a necessary evil, she had said to him. She wanted a house of her own, maybe even another kid. How did he think they were going to manage that, the way things were now? She had asked him to tell her what *he* wanted. Could he at least tell her that? But Jerry couldn't. He'd tried being evasive, talked about the risks of investing.

"These guys aren't doing us any favours. There's always something in it for them."

"I'm not saying there isn't," Sarah had said. "There's

something in it for the banks too, but I don't hear you complaining about them."

Finally, she'd told him simply not to screw things up. She'd told him not to get up to his usual tricks.

"So, where exactly does our money go?" Sarah asked.

"A thousand places," Helen said. "That's the beauty."

"Who's it hurting?" Jerry asked.

"What do you mean, son?" Arthur asked.

Sarah said, "He means are we contributing to child labour or the destruction of the rainforest?"

"You can't breathe these days without doing *some* damage," Arthur said. "The portfolios will tell you what you want to know about that."

The sound of Anna's crying drifted down the stairs to the dining room. Jerry excused himself. Sarah gave him another look. "Don't fall asleep again, Van Winkle," she said.

Jerry turned the corner toward the stairs. He climbed the steps to the second floor. Anna was sitting up in bed, crying and holding on to her blanket. He picked her up. "Hey, sweetheart," Jerry said. "Did you wake up?" He held her to his chest and walked around the room. "Did someone leave you all alone?"

That morning, Jerry had gone into the supply room to get dry ink for the history department's photocopier. It was the office where the young temp worked. The supply room was no bigger than a closet, but it was out of view of the main office, so as he was turning to leave she'd come up to him and kissed him quickly on the lips. She might have been kissing him goodbye at a party or seeing him off at the airport, the kiss had been that light and swift. Out of habit, he had put his arm around her waist, long enough to pull her close, as he always did with Sarah. It was like slipping on another jacket, as though his body had no memory of the hundreds of nights he'd slept beside Sarah. In the seconds after the kiss, he'd wondered what the point of marriage *was* if it could crumble so quickly at the touch of another person. What was the *point*? Were we really nothing more than six year olds sneaking into the cloakroom when the teacher's back was turned? The woman had left without saying a word and so had he. It was just a *kiss*. That was why he'd held out his glass for more wine and why he'd fallen asleep beside Anna, wishing his life into oblivion. In the dining room, Sarah was planning their future and above her head he was thinking of ways to blow it to pieces.

Through the Underwoods' bedroom window, Jerry saw a light go on next door at his house. Shadows moved across the yellow rectangle in the basement suite. His watch read 1:30. They must be getting up to eat.

Anna had fallen back to sleep. Jerry laid her on the bed and covered her up. It was probably the liquor, but everything he looked at seemed terribly strained: the stuffed animal he squeezed into Anna's hand, the bedcovers he pulled up under her chin. He was amazed how tawdry life had become.

He descended the stairs. Sarah's voice sounded angry. There was a hint of impatience rising to the surface, too. "Look at this list," she was saying. "This is a prospectus?"

Instead of turning back into the dining room, he found himself opening the front door and walking down the front steps to the lawn. Something caught his ankle and sent him sprawling. The quiet of the night fell around him. Nobody had heard him. He got to his feet and crossed through the flower bed that divided the Underwoods' property from their own. He walked up the path that led around to the backyard until he came to the window he had seen from the bedroom. The glass was steamed with condensation. Behind him he heard Helen Underwood calling his name and then Sarah too. Before long all three of them were yelling for him. He put his fingers onto the window's surface. He could feel the heat from the kitchen, almost smell pepper and coriander through the glass. Beads of water rolled down the misted pane in rivers. He could make out thin ribbons of life on the other side: a beaded curtain, some fridge magnets shaped like flowers, the eyes of a girl looking out at him from a painting. Somebody crossed from one side of the room to the other.

Sarah's voice sounded closer now.

"Jerry?" she asked, behind him. "What are you *doing*?"

"Shhh," he said. He'd been hoping for more time. He hadn't seen anything yet.

# TOO BUSY
# SWIMMING

The Scotsman's Palace is a no-star, plaid-trimmed, stucco motel on a busy road in the industrial district. I could have chosen a B&B by the park, or a room at the Save Inn, but the Palace fit the Victoria School Board's budget. It was close to a mall and away from all the tourist kitsch by the harbour. Teachers stayed there for conferences because it was cheap; they could save a few bucks on their per diem.

It was nearly midnight by the time I walked into the lobby. It had taken me five hours to cover 60 miles. In five hours I could have flown to Toronto. When I lived in Victoria, friends from the mainland always asked if I felt trapped living on an island. Now I understood the question. The clerk gave me a room overlooking the street, across from an all-night coffeeshop crowded with taxi drivers and hookers. The coffeeshop offered a breakfast deal for Palace guests.

In the morning, I called Doreen in Vancouver, then got a booth. Leona was already at the counter waiting for me. For a few months one winter, I had imagined leaving Doreen for her. She was one of those bullets a man has to dodge, and I did, but only just. If anybody knew my taste in accommodation, Leona did.

"How's it feel to be so predictable?" she said, standing up.

"Good," I said. Leona was a counsellor in Smithers, but four years earlier we were both teachers at the same school in Victoria. I caught the waiter's eye, made the international sign for coffee and walked with Leona over to a table by the window.

"Nice day for a deposition," I said.

"Days, you mean," she said

"I was hoping you wouldn't say that." The waiter brought two coffees and a couple of menus.

"There's 35 of us on the list, Tony. You'll be lucky to see Doreen by Christmas."

"I don't have that much to say," I said.

"You'll say whatever it takes," she said. "I've been waiting 10 years for this."

I ordered *huevos rancheros*. Leona had the waffles. Rain slipped down the glass. The summer drought was finally over. Two kids were looking under the hood of a car in the jobber's parking lot on the corner. One of them was holding a set of ignition wires and pointing, while the other one twisted something back and forth.

"Doreen's doing another burn," I said. "She was going to come with me, see some old friends, but the boss phoned her when his bid was accepted."

"That's too bad," Leona said. "I guess you'll just have to make do." The people at the next table settled into their sausages, eggs and pancakes; aromas mingled in the air.

"I'm not looking forward to this," I said.

"You'll be fine, Tony," she said.

"That's what Doreen said." On the far side of the room, a large-screen television flickered silently.

"Did you hear they found the guy who fell off the ferry?" she asked.

"I was just telling Doreen on the phone I thought I saw him. It was in the paper," I said.

"Oh, yeah? They had him on the news. He said God saved him from drowning."

"Funny how God saves drunks, but forgets about the starving in Ethiopia."

"Same old Tony," Leona said.

With the fire on Mason Street, Doreen knew she had overtime for weeks. It became clear I'd have to testify on my own. Work is work and when it comes she has to take it. I'm a teacher. I stand up all day in front of an audience, but still I was nervous about what lay ahead. Anybody who thinks it's easy should try it some time.

We were out to dinner at the Cohens, friends through Doreen's book club who live off West 13th in a trendy brick walk-up, when Doreen got the call. Half the time Ellen Cohen never makes it to the club. Her kids are young; it was just wishful thinking. She has no time to read. Doreen says Ellen hasn't finished a book yet. Every so often, we bring over a lasagne, a casserole, or a big salad from our garden. It's the least we can do, Doreen says, not having any kids ourselves. We didn't decide not to have children, but it *was* our decision not to make fools of ourselves tracking down every herbal remedy and surgical option on the market. People say children are the glue that keeps a couple together. Maybe we're all the more amazing, then, living under the same roof without the benefit of adhesives. Or maybe it's just a matter of time.

Dinner was finished and Doreen was giving me her look, the one that tells me I'm dominating conversation. I was telling Sam about a boy in my class who'd found his older brother shot in his living room. "The news said the kid shot himself 'to death,'"

I was saying. "Have you ever heard anything so *stupid*?"

"Well, he did, didn't he?" Sam asked.

"That's not the point," I said. "You'd think the guy was just sitting there on the sofa plugging away until he was so full of lead he finally died. All they needed to say was he shot himself."

"What if he shoots himself and misses?" Sam asked.

"First they told us he committed suicide," I said. "Then they told us he shot himself to death. It's just a bit much. That's all I'm saying."

I didn't tell Sam it was Doreen who had cleaned up the living room after the boy's brother shot himself. It's not the sort of thing people think is covered by insurance, but it often is. After the police give the go ahead, a counsellor informs the family that they're free to call in professionals if their policy allows for it. If not, it's out of their own pockets, or they do it themselves. Doreen was there for three days. The carpet and sofa were too far gone, but even if they hadn't been, nobody would have felt comfortable in the same room with them again. What took her the time was the other furniture: the big English sideboard, the walnut coffee table, all the end tables and paintings. You can't be dusting and come upon a splotch of blood. And the walls and ceiling weren't easy either. Blood goes right through most paint, so all of it had to come off before they could spray. She found bits of bone and brain all the way into the dining room.

When the pager beeped, Doreen excused herself to use the phone and gave me "the look" again. She does it while fixing her hair. She's never really said, "When I do this, you stop talking," it's just that she gets so fed up she has to do *something*. I shut up and let Sam talk about his boy's soccer game. In the car on the way home, Doreen said, "You'll be fine."

"Like a rock," I said.

Four years ago, Doreen was with Clean All Services in Victoria, doing flooded basement suites ruined in the big rains of '92. I was a substitute with the district, teaching a "Gifted Eights" program at Douglas Junior Secondary. When I got offered permanent work with a school in Vancouver, we moved. We were still thinking about kids of our own and a permanent job was part of the plan.

At Douglas, two teachers ran the outdoor education program as well as taught drama classes. One was lean and tall, meticulous, the other squat like a bowling ball and very casual. Everybody called them Abbott and Costello. I didn't know them well, but occasionally I had coffee with them in the Green Room before classes. They'd fixed the place up with some worn-out living room furniture, a few dusty armchairs and a long chesterfield. The atmosphere was more hospitable than in the staff room, which still reeked from years of smoke. Drama students came and went, hanging out, doing their homework, reading magazines. Leona and another counsellor had been telling the principal for years the whole thing was a scam. They said Abbott and Costello had their own female fan club, that the drama was just an excuse to stay after school. They said the outdoor education kids went on field trips to a cabin and ate popcorn and massaged the teachers' necks. When the principal retired, the district started asking questions. Anybody who'd seen anything got a call. The formal depositions were the last step. Both of them were going to be in the room with us while we told the jury what we knew. That was the part I wasn't happy about.

Doreen's fire turned out to be a bad one: nobody hurt, but plenty of water and smoke damage. We'd seen the headline and driven by the next day. For Doreen, every fire's a potential work site — a black job, they call it — so she takes an active interest. The flames had blown out a basement window and a screen door was off its hinges. The owners, a couple, were standing on the front lawn. The woman was holding a sweater with a black line right across its front.

"I'll be back," Doreen said as we drove off.

"You think so?" I asked.

"If I'm lucky," she said.

Doreen's is the biggest cleaning contractor in the southern mainland, used by all the insurance companies. She's done everything from sewer ruptures to multiple murders in the past three years and her reputation is stellar.

When I phoned her from the Scotsman's Palace to see how things were going, she said, "It's not the write-off the owners want it to be. Yesterday, they came in to look at a fridge I'd cleaned. They said that it wasn't safe, that there were cracks in the lining and to move it to the discard pile. They even tried to bribe me."

"Get out," I said.

"It's true."

They didn't know Doreen. She will clean a blouse 10 times before she gives up on it.

"So, what are you going to do?" I asked.

"Don't you worry about that," she said.

Jerry, Doreen's boss, has more faith in her than he does in God and he's a Pentecostal. When she says something is safe, he doesn't need a second opinion. He tells the clients that, as far as he's concerned, the case is closed. Usually they back right down.

"Did you read about that guy in the paper?" I asked her.

"I'm a working girl, Tony," she said. "I don't have time to read."

"I saw him, Doreen."

"Saw who?"

"The guy on the ferry," I said. "The one who fell off."

"You saw a guy fall off the ferry?"

"No, I saw the guy before he fell off the ferry. I went back to my car to get my briefcase and he was standing on the car deck, leaning over the rail. He was throwing up."

"Nice," she said.

"Eleven hours he was in the strait. Can you imagine? The paper said he'd lost his balance while he was throwing up. That's got to be the same guy."

"Eleven hours," she said. "It'd be ugly."

"He was still alive," I said.

"Lucky drunk."

"The paper said it was sunstroke. He'd been playing softball at a picnic."

"Sure," Doreen said.

"Yeah," I said. "*His* wife didn't sound convinced either."

Doreen said the man needed to "dry out." She said she had to go to the warehouse even though it was a Saturday. Jerry's a slave driver when there's work on the table. The movers bring in the burnt goods and Doreen and the other staff clean what they can and put it in storage. More than three fires in one week and they're out of storage space, so Jerry likes to move things along pretty quickly. He gives them whatever they need to get the job done: industrial washing machines, rubber gloves, 45-gallon drums of carbon tetrachloride. Doreen lives down there when a whole house comes in. The only time she gets out is for floods or murders.

After breakfast with Leona, I walked up to the Executive House. The board had rented a couple of seminar rooms on the 10th floor for deposing witnesses. They also had a suite where people could wait until it was their turn. Leona was right. I'd been scheduled for eleven o'clock, but at this rate anything before two was out of the question. The suite was jammed with coats and briefcases. Somebody had thought to bring in a couple of Mr. Coffee machines, so the bedside tables were littered with empty sugar packets and spilled whitener. There were teachers from a dozen different schools, people who had transferred or moved out of town and returned to the scene of the crime. I moved to the window and looked out at the Empress, oak trees and Douglas firs in Beacon Hill Park. Behind me, the board rep was talking to the next witness, Wayne Evans, a science teacher.

"We'll be asking the questions," the rep was saying, "so there's nothing to worry about. We already know what you know. You just have to tell it the way you remember it."

"Do *they* ask questions too?" Wayne asked.

"There is no cross-examination," the rep said. "We are just gathering evidence. They're allowed to be here, but they can't interfere."

A few minutes later, a clerk came in to tell us they were adjourning until two o'clock. Anybody who hadn't been deposed yet should return tomorrow. I put on my coat and left.

I walked down the causeway to Belleville and along the waterfront into James Bay. If the term had been further along, I'd have brought some marking. I was hoping I wouldn't need the substitute I'd booked for Monday.

I strolled out to the navigation beacon at the end of the breakwater. Two kids had planted themselves on one of its stone slabs and were casting their lines into a kelp bed. Somebody had packed them a lunch. Two bright orange Thermoses stood beside a tackle box and a couple of Tupperware containers lay next to them, the clean-cut corners of white bread sandwiches visible through transparent lids. They tugged on their lures, reeled in their lines, eyes fixed on the water. Seagulls bobbed nearby, jockeying for handouts. The remnants of a Friday-night beach fire smouldered among some logs by the shore, its smoke married to the wind and the mist. I went back the way I'd come, past Chinatown and across Bay to the Scotsman's Palace, where I'd said I'd meet Leona.

I phoned Doreen that evening to tell her about the delay. She had taken the portable into the bath with her and the sound of water slapping against the tub made me think she was trapped in a bottle of pop.

"Some people should not have house fires," she said.

"Doreen," I said. "Do you know what you just said?"

"No, I mean it," she said. "These people are rude. They want the insurance company to buy them a whole new life. They're pulling garbage from the attic and want me to say it needs replacing. Jeans they wore out five years ago, junky old typewriters nobody'll ever use again. Garbage, in anybody's book."

"Some people are sentimental," I said.

"And some people are perverts," she said. "You don't want to know what kind of pictures I found in some of their books. I could go to the police with what I've seen."

"No, really?" I said.

"Some with kids," she said.

In one fire, the movers had brought in a couple's matching

coffins to be cleaned, homemade ones from kits. They were covered in signatures and messages from friends. There were even circular wine stains on them, as if they'd been used as coffee tables for a party. Doreen is always coming home with this stuff. I thought about the small bag of dope I had tucked away in my desk drawer, sex toys we had tried and then relegated to a box under the bathroom sink. Would I want a cleaning contractor joking to his wife about that? I resolved to throw everything out as soon as I got home.

"I saw your guy too," Doreen said.

"My guy?"

"Yeah. Your drunken ferry guy. He was on TV."

"You mean my Christian drunken ferry guy," I said.

"That's the one. He was going over his route on a map. Some cop fishing near the American border picked him up."

"What was he using for bait?" I asked.

"His wife was interviewed too," she said. "She was holding her husband's pager up to the camera. The thing still worked after 11 hours in the water."

"He had his pager with him?"

"His wife tried to phone him when he didn't show up. He remembers the call, but he said there wasn't a lot he could do about it at the time. He was too busy swimming."

"Aren't we all," I said.

The next day, the inquiry was back on schedule. I went over early to look through my daybook again, the one I'd kept from that year at the school. There wasn't a lot of detail, but I wanted to be sure of the dates.

I knew what they would be looking for. That year my class was invited to participate in an orienteering exercise with the outdoor education kids. It was my first class, so I wanted to make it a year they wouldn't forget. We turned the outing into an overnight camping expedition. I divided the students into groups, made them responsible for their dinners, had them set up budgets, create supply lists. Doreen offered to come along. Every "learning outcome" was covered. The day of the trip, everything went as planned. We took the school bus along the island highway and up into the wooded hills behind Shawnigan Lake. When we came to a narrow gravel road, all of us put on our backpacks and hiked the last two miles to the cabin. It was fall, the mornings just turning frosty. Each group made a fire pit and sent foragers off for dry wood. In the evening, the students gathered for hot chocolate and cookies and one of the teachers, Costello probably, played guitar and sang. When it was over, I called lights out and the kids went to their tents for the night. Students weren't supposed to go into the cabin except for the evening sing-song, but the girls figured out they could if they were pretty and if they didn't mind sitting in front of the fire with a teacher's arm draped over their shoulders. Plain Janes didn't make it past the front door.

The morning after, Doreen sat beside me and closed the magazine I'd been reading. She was the girls' chaperone. She told me she was going to walk back into town and phone every one of the parents and tell them to come and collect their kids right away if I didn't do something. She said she'd never seen anything so disgusting in her whole life and if this was an education it was the kind nobody needed.

In the week following the camp, I wrote down what had happened. I tore up what I had written and wrote it again. I tore that up too. I imagined conversations between me and the principal, between me and the counsellors. Leona got it out of me in her usual way and she nearly hit the roof. She wanted blood. It was the last straw, she kept saying, but I wasn't so sure. In the end, I went and talked to Abbott privately. I told him what I'd seen. I said it was our job to be models of proper behaviour. He nodded. He agreed. He understood completely. He even thanked me for bringing the problem to his attention. He said it would never happen again.

Now it was my turn to give evidence. The board representative led me out of the suite and down a hall to the seminar room. He showed me to a chair at the front of the room. I sat down. A panel of people had taken up positions behind a table opposite me. A few of them stared at a point somewhere behind my head. Others kept their eyes averted and wrote on legal pads, their pens pausing the way birds pause from time to time when they're feeding, alert to any changes around them. To my left, behind a table of his own, stood Abbott, a lawyer at his side. He acknowledged me with a nod I did not return. The board representative read a prepared text for my benefit. It explained the purpose of the proceedings and the manner in which they would be conducted. Then, one by one, the members of the panel, as though they were speaking lines from a play, began to ask questions.

# SOMETIMES
# NIGHT NEVER
# ENDS

"I won't relax 'til we get there," Wendy says.

"Thanks for the warning," Allan says. The oil light blinks out, then reappears briefly, the Volvo's way of saying good luck. In the back seat, Claire and Alex struggle with the seat belts.

"Too many gas stations," says Wendy. "And tow trucks. I really hate the tow trucks. Always some wiseguy in tight jeans."

"Did you bring matches?" asks Allan.

"Yes. And the dogfood."

"Your problem is you never remember the days we *don't* break down. When was the last time I was under the hood? Five thousand miles ago. Nearly a year. We could've gone to Montreal and back by now."

"My point exactly," says Wendy. "We're due."

Pumpkins on the neighbours' porches. Dark already and only 5:30.

"But it's really 6:30. Right, Dad?" says Claire.

Yesterday Allan went through the house changing all the clocks. With a globe and a flashlight, he showed her the Earth tilting away, how sometimes night never ends in the north. "The Eskimos must have long dreams," Claire said.

In the rearview mirror, Allan watches the Volvo's steamy exhaust fill the street. Invisible balloons follow at their heels, exploding with muffled bangs, three, sometimes four, at once. Sirens too, ending in a thunderclap. Can't blame the noise on the car this time. Ghosts parade up sidewalks. Jack-o'-lanterns stand guard in windows, at front doors. Every once in a while, a dark house, curtains drawn tight across the front windows. The faint glow of a lamp through cloth suggests somebody might be lying low, ignoring the doorbell, a self-imposed blackout.

"Brutus is shivering," Alex says, petting the dog's fur, rubbing his jowls, smoothing his flattened ears.

"Keep his head down," Allan says. "We'll be out of town soon."

Growing up in their parents' stucco split level, Allan and his sisters celebrated October's end taking turns at the living room window, peeking out from behind the curtain at goblins running down their street, bags of loot rubbing against crepe paper and old sheets. Some would stop at the gate, weigh the odds, even try the latch. But no one ever came as far as the porch. Those who knew walked right by, but one or two whose parents had a particular gripe shouted names as they passed. "Dumb Jehovahs."

"You just don't like the way it looks," Allan says. "I know a guy who does body work, cheap."

"Paint's not going to help if the clutch goes," Wendy says.

"Look! Policemen!" shouts Alex. A heritage group complained loudly about the vandalism in Memorial Cemetery last year. They blamed Satanists, teenagers and winos. This year spotlights twist through the trees and over mausoleums and patrol cars flash blue and red along neat, curbless graveyard roads.

"They kill cats and dogs," says Claire, meaning the devil worshippers.

"Not ours, they don't," says Allan. The car picks up speed as it veers onto the highway, past the last drive-in theatre in town.

"Just think, if we kept driving," Allan says, "we could catch the ferry at Kelsey Bay, the one to Rupert and open ocean, the swell of tides coming in from Japan."

"I'm not falling for it, Allan. Dream on." The lane to their right swerves off into the trees.

Seventy miles. Allan flicks the signal indicator and opens his window for the upcoming right turn, his arm ready. Force of habit; can't trust those blinkers. The pavement narrows, streetlights disappear. One of the Volvo's high beams shoots up into the black sky.

Allan stopped going to the Kingdom Hall a year after he got married. "Unevenly yoked," the elders said when Wendy declined for the last time to accept the truth of Jehovah: tribulation, Armageddon, the new world. The Witnesses disfellowshipped him, cut him off from all contact with the congregation. Shunned: the standard punishment for smokers, adulterers, skeptics. The last time he talked to any of his sisters was 10 years ago. Letters to his mother still come back unopened. Allan closed his eyes, hung on, like Jacob. He let the anger burn until it flaked away like sunburned skin, tender underneath, healing. Along the narrow country road, the darkened houses look scarier than those with black cats in their windows or skeletons dancing on their porches.

When they arrive, Allan opens the driver's door and crosses in front of the headlights to unlock the gate, crosses back again, waving, a hero for driving them the last 40 feet to the cabin. Four doors yawn at once, then the trunk: a loaded jack-in-the-box. Bags and baskets parade up the steps, everybody's in the spotlight now. Just in case, Allan walks through the door first. He finds the lights, the hot water tank, kindling for the stove. Three dead mice under the sink this time. The kids claim the same beds they've had for the past eight years.

"Lots of dry branches out here for the bonfire," says Allan as he heads back outside. "Help me drag them to the pile." The beam from his flashlight bobs along the ground, settling on thick fir boughs downed by the big snowfall.

"You always make it too big," Wendy shouts into the night. Brutus explores the patchwork of animal scents: raccoon, deer, maybe another dog. He noses around the perimeter of the cabin, tracking creatures that have passed by.

"Start cutting the onions," Allan says.

Later, in the kitchen, Alex claims it is his turn to draw the pumpkin's face. Wendy gives him the pencil, says he can do the eyes and nose, Claire the mouth. Wendy's reflection hovers in the skylight, watches over her shoulder while Alex constructs triangles. A black reflection, warped in the Plexiglas, still unblemished by rain.

"Take it easy on the jalapeños tonight," says Wendy. Allan looks up from untying his boots. Brutus curls into his place under the cookstove. "I want the kids to eat."

"So, no peppers," Allan says.

"Why do you do that?" she asks. "I only said to take it easy. Don't make me feel guilty for asking. Maybe you can put peppers just in ours. I don't know."

"Did you cut the onions?" Allan asks.

"I was helping them with the pumpkin." Wendy pulls the cutlery drawer open too far.

"Not too hot," he says, coming to her aid. "I promise." Knives and forks. Spoons too. Like pick-up sticks all over the floor. They kiss over a potato peeler, lift the drawer together.

Allan starts whistling as soon as he picks up a knife, dances between counter and stove, stirring, shaking, a vaudeville plate spinner. No recipe. One clove, maybe four. Or 10. He doesn't own measuring spoons. The oil's hot enough when his spit bounces back at him. Lining them up's the best part. Drag another tortilla screaming from the pan, down the conveyor belt of beef mix, hot sauce and cheese. Roll 'em up. Squeeze 'em. Minutes pass like enchiladas, like soldiers, like pepper falling from the mill. Wine spills onto cast iron, shimmering hot, wine steam, wine rain, wine sweat. The cabin's silence is broken by flaming mouthfuls of grape, eruptions of boiling oil, four armloads of good dry fir. It's a coven of swirling wood smoke, rich peasant food, a kitchen tempest spinning around and around the whistling magician at its core.

Many Jehovah's Witnesses do something else for Hallowe'en. Chinese food. Or a movie. Anything to escape the house for the night. Even after the church had expelled Allan, he and Wendy made it a habit to be away from the house October 31st. "Just because I stopped one bit of foolishness doesn't mean I have to start another," Allan said. Once they camped at Hurricane Ridge. That was the time the Volvo quit outside Port Angeles.

When Claire was born, Wendy's parents offered them their cabin. Not really *close*, but only a two-hour drive. They made it a tradition. Three years into their second child now, Allan's *Watchtower* fears of plastic devils and cardboard witches have been eclipsed by less theoretical horrors: a seven year old, two fingers gone after a spark dropped into his bag of firecrackers; the neighbour's missing girl, found the next morning and taken to hospital stiff with strychnine; poisoned candy; booby-trapped fruit.

"The lamps are empty," Wendy says. Cheese flutters down, snow on lava.

"Kerosene's in the shed," Allan says. "Behind the chainsaw. I'm just finished."

"Smells wonderful," she says, "They'll look prettier than candles".

⌗

The roof over the customs wicket at the Port Angeles ferry terminal was flat and wide, long enough for five cars to be processed at one time. The agent didn't have to leave his seat; most of the time he asked questions through a sliding window. Allan and Wendy had chosen Hurricane Ridge because they hadn't been to the States before. They had chosen it because the lights of Port Angeles were visible nearly every night from the beach at the foot of their street. Some red ones, the occasional blue one, a meagre rainbow at the foot of the Olympic Mountains.

"Camping this time of year?" the agent said. A working town, full of taverns, loggers and shore workers.

"Need to get away," said Allan.

The agent said, "Better check with the ranger on the road in. He likes to know who's where."

They picked up some cold beer at a Safeway and stopped at Penny's for a pair of blue work shirts. "Prison blue," the clerk said. Allan had to shift into second as they climbed toward the ridge, the valley on their left more mist than trees.

"This hill doesn't give up," said Allan. Brutus's nose brushed past Allan's left ear, sniffed mountain wind, feet fighting for balance on the back seat. The late-afternoon sun brought out a few marmots, tawny brown, still a bit of summer fat. No snow yet. "How can you look at this," Allan said, "and not believe in God?"

Ranger Dan told them he would bend a little because they were Canadians, but normally the campsite was closed after September 30th. In the night, Allan woke up Wendy, his arm rigid beside hers, clutching a Bowie knife under his pillow. He'd heard something. They didn't close their eyes until dawn.

Halfway down the next morning, the timing gear went. Stripped. Push rods bent. Crankshaft seized. No compression to slow them down. At the bottom, Allan got out to check the brakes. The heat had melted all the axle grease, covered the rims, the tires. A truck towed them to the ferry.

"Last sailing's the best I can do," said the ticket agent. "We'll have to push you on."

Eleven hours under the customs roof. Sleeping. Kissing sometimes. Listening to the radio. After five Wendy called it torture. "Is it our fault the stupid engine won't work?" said Wendy. "I bet they make cripples pay more."

#

The bonfire refuses to light. Four chairs balance in a semicircle around a thin stream of smoke. Expectant, optimistic. Allan tips back a bottle of wine, his glass forgotten on the kitchen table, peppers bubbling inside him.

Wendy prods a wad of smouldering newspaper, sinks to her knees and blows.

"Cedar shavings any help?" Allan asks.

"I don't see why I should have to do this," she says. "You make all the other fires."

"Division of labour. I cook, you light the bonfire. Good example for the kids."

"Good example, oh sure," says Wendy, adding more shavings, another copy of the *Times*.

"Can we light a sparkler now?" asks Claire.

"Sure, sweetheart," says Allan. "Matches, dear?"

"I'm out."

The ground betrays Allan as he gropes his way up the small hill to the house.

"OK there, big fella?" asks Wendy.

"Tripped," Allan says.

On his way back down, Allan makes a detour and grabs the tin of coal oil from behind the chainsaw. A peanut butter jar full, the recommended amount for recalcitrant bonfires. Kerosene. Jet fuel, thinks Allan dimly. Little men out on the wings, stoking the flames a glass at a time. He's a sleepwalker with nitroglycerine crossing a stage of fallen logs, slick grass.

"Didn't spill a drop," he says.

"What?" asks Wendy.

"Stand back," says Allan. "Show time."

Claire, Alex, Wendy, a triptych of doubt, barely visible outside the circle of dull cindery light. In the centre, a single small flame, enough for Allan to find the bottle again. Kerosene in his left hand, wine in his right. He drinks one and tosses the other into the fire.

High on a stick, aluminum flash powder explodes for the man under the cape. Still life. Etched on Allan's cornea. Hold it. Wendy's mouth a perfect *O*. The mushroom blast. The end of time. Children peeking from behind long skirts, through curtains, the last moment before skin lifts, flakes, crumbles into dust.

The magician bows, fire crackling its applause.

"That is probably the stupidest thing I've ever seen you do," says Wendy.

Allan lifts his hands, palms outward, magnanimous in victory.

&#9291;

In bed they watch the ceiling, the last few logs of the bonfire casting shadows on window panes and planks of red cedar. They tremble, pulse, like Wendy's hand. Allan realizes he's forgotten to turn back his watch. Only 1:15, then. He thinks of the world tilting into icy perpetual dark. Rain comes without warning, the tin roof erupts into a long hiss, a gramophone as the steel needle first strikes the groove. For a second, the fire grows bright, then brighter still.

# PIG ON A SPIT

"That's a strange-looking stamp," Bill Spears says. He and Peter Mayhew are looking down at a stack of mail in the Hope Bay General Store/Canada Post Outlet/Liquor Distribution Branch. A pale blue airmail envelope bearing Peter's name and address sits on top.

"It's Italian," Peter says.

"Imagine that," Bill says.

And because courtesy and privacy are unheard of in a community this small and because Peter is useless at hiding things anyway, he communicates to Bill Spears — and thus to every permanent and part-time resident of Tuckerman's Island — the skimpy contents of the travel-weary envelope, his ex-wife's cryptic jottings, his son's thin question.

"Shit," Bill says, which is what he says to any news, good or bad.

"Shit is right," Peter agrees.

"Probably a good thing," Bill offers a moment later.

"Good for whom?" Peter asks.

Bill Spears shakes his head. In sympathy or disgust, Peter can't really tell which. He leafs through his mail. A subscription renewal to a Montreal magazine, two direct-mail charity appeals and a GST refund cheque for $64.03. He pockets both cheque and letter and drops everything else into a recycling container underneath the bank of mailboxes.

"I have blackberries to pick," he says and leaves.

In Paris's fifth *arrondissement*, just east of a carefully maintained park called Le Jardin des Plantes, is a small mosque that serves mint tea most afternoons. Unobtrusive, black-jacketed waiters place glasses of honey-sweetened tea on tables almost as soon as customers sit down. They are escaping Paris traffic, piles of dog shit and people with cameras. In a whitewashed courtyard, under umbrellas, men and women speak in low voices or smoke cigarettes or sip their tea and admire a flourishing olive tree. David Mayhew, age 13, sits with his mother. They talk as they have learned to talk in their time together, alternating staccato bursts with silence.

"I won't need my skate," he says.

"Child of all children," she says.

He rolls his eyes. "You said," he says and drains his glass of tea.

"I know, I know," she says. "I forgot." She takes a franc from her purse, the penalty for embarrassing endearments, and pushes it across to him.

"If it rains . . . ," he begins to say.

"Oh, it rains, David," she says. "It rains."

Later they walk back to the Hotel Monge that has been their home for the last week of their European holiday. They buy sparkling water and mangoes at a corner *marché* and catch up on news and sports on their hotel TV.

After a while, David asks her to go with him to watch a group of skateboarders around a fountain in a large square. The performers wear cargo pants and logo-laden T-shirts and entertain crowds with complicated flips and jumps and grinds. She listens to David's commentary, sometimes critical, sometimes approving.

In two days, she will go with him to Charles de Gaulle Airport. She will put him on a plane to Canada's West Coast. She will stay on another day to catch her connection to Palm Springs. A man who was once her client will meet her there and they will get married. She cut the man's hair for three years, listened to him talk about his kids, his divorce, his job. When he hired a barbershop quartet to sing his proposal, she accepted.

But David didn't. Europe was supposed to ease the transition, but it has been a month of argument, a campaign by David to talk her out of remarriage. *This guy's a jerk. I can't talk to him. He hates me.* And now her ex-husband has agreed to meet David in Vancouver and take him to his Gulf Island home for a couple of weeks. She wrote to Peter only because her son had asked her to — it was a way he could cause her pain. He was wrong, of course. As long as David is alive and healthy, there is nothing he can do to hurt her.

Two weeks ago in Pisa, she surprised him, told him to dictate and she'd write the letter. She thought she'd called his bluff. He blinked, but didn't back down. She sat on a chair by a window looking over a sea of terra cotta roofs and grapevines. He lay back on his sagging twin bed and told her what to say:

> *Dad,*
>
> *I know I haven't visited you in a long time (Mom says four years), but would it be okay if I came and stayed with you? I could help you get firewood and stuff like that if you want.*
>
> *Sincerely,*
> *David*

On a separate page, she filled in dates, times, flight numbers. Nothing personal. No explanations.

Upon their arrival in Paris, a single-sentence reply, scrawled on hotel stationery by some night clerk: "I'll be waiting — Dad."

Peter Mayhew pours hot wax into one of 15 moulds that have been hand formed in a large box of sand. Embedded in each mould is a piece of driftwood chosen for its artful curve, its grain, its weathered West Coast charm. When they cool, sand and wax and wood will form a Fern Island Candle®. Sunset yellows, oranges and reds decorate each candle's single sandless face, which, along with a delicate branch of fern, lends a tropical touch when the wick is lit. People call them "magic lanterns." Bay stores across Canada have ordered thousands. Local craft fairs involve months of production. Peter's neighbour, Kent Isbister, learned how to make the candles from a Hawaiian entrepreneur who has now retired with his profits. Kent hires local islanders such as Peter to cart sand up to his workshop, keep wax boiling on a three-burner propane stove, drill holes in freshly cast candles and insert wicks. Kent used to do these jobs himself, but now he is too busy. He has a cell phone to keep in touch with agents. He coordinates pickup and delivery. He orders wax. When he's not on his phone, he's an artist. He alone composes each candle's polychromatic face. Using a palette of wax crayons, Kent melts mystery into every candle, sometimes evoking a face or an animal, but always infusing a glow that people say reminds them of stained glass.

Kent enjoys having a poet working for him. He thinks Peter Mayhew lends his business greater integrity. Kent has never read anything Peter has written. He has only heard rumours of his public drunkenness, his violent temper and a family abandoned.

Kent likes to imagine he himself could have been a Peter Mayhew. In his youth, he wrote poems and stormed about in a rage like Peter. Even now he gets angry when orders aren't filled or wax shipments fail to appear. Ferry delays send him into a fury. Still, he can't imagine what would compel a man to live in a two-room shack without running water or electricity. And halfway up a mountain yet, on a logging road inaccessible to cars. Kent has heard another rumour, that Peter's 13-year-old son is coming for a visit after four years away. So he's tolerant when Peter comes over to tell him he's unable to work this Wednesday.

"No problem," Kent says. "We can ease up for a day."

"Good," Peter says. He picks up a stack of pre-labelled decorator boxes for shipping and turns away.

"You should bring him up for a look around," Kent says.

"Who's that?" Peter asks over his shoulder.

"Your son."

"Why would I do that?"

"Show him what you do, I guess."

"This isn't what I do," Peter says and walks away.

A French Canadian flight attendant shows David to his seat. David has spent 20 minutes looking at flight controls and maps with a boy from first class who was also invited on a tour of flight CP-151's cockpit. They learned that, currently, they and their fellow passengers are out of range of conventional ground radar and that, because most pilots once flew fighter planes, they find domestic air traffic repetitive and very boring. David is not sure why they were told these things. Nothing of what he heard has consoled him about potential mid-air collisions or engine failure. He asks for a packet of peanuts, but is given pretzels. The risk of an allergic reaction is too great.

Captain Lawson also mentioned they would soon pass over Uranium City in northern Saskatchewan, so David searches through an *En Route* magazine to see how close to Kamloops their flight path takes them. Kamloops is not shown on any map in the magazine, but David can see where it would be, which isn't far out of their way. He finds it strange he will pass over his own town, leave it behind. Eight years ago, he and his mother moved, first to Vancouver and then to Kamloops, where his mother got a loan to go to hairdressing school. This was after she divorced his dad. Now she has her own shop on Tranquille Road near Safeway. For a few years, David visited his father on the island, but when an RCMP officer phoned his mother to tell her David had been found in a rowboat by himself, drifting near a ferry route at eleven o'clock in the morning, she cut off all communication with his father.

A man next to David is telling him not to worry. He is telling David that he was once an air traffic controller himself and that odds of a crash are very low. David wasn't aware he appeared frightened. He wants to look at himself in a mirror to see if he can see what alerted the man, but all the bathrooms are occupied. His neighbour speaks quickly. He has an accent too, but David has no idea what it is.

"You were too young," the man says, "but back in '84 Ronald Reagan fired all the air traffic controllers. Fired them, just like that." He is perspiring despite a cool breeze descending on them from vents overhead.

"Why did he do that?" David asks.

"They were greedy," the man says. "Stupid too. They wanted more money, more time off, early-retirement packages. They thought they had government negotiators by the balls. Air traffic was an essential service, they thought. Who'd be crazy enough to fire them? So they went on strike. Maybe they wanted a holiday. Maybe some guy wanted to be at his daughter's wedding and he needed time off. Who knows? But you know what?"

"No," David says.

"Reagan wasn't as nuts as people say he was," the man says.

"He wasn't?" David asks, though he's not really sure who Reagan is.

"Not a bit," the man says. "The controllers were so full of themselves they went on strike right at the beginning of summer. They thought all the people who'd booked vacation flights would be so pissed off they'd force the government to give in after a week or two. But it backfired on them."

"How?" David asks.

"It was summer, for Christ's sake! Not a cloud in the sky! Anybody with two eyes in his head could've been a controller in that weather. If they'd struck in December or January, with all the snow and rain, the strike wouldn't have lasted an hour. Reagan knew that. So he fired them all and brought in the military. By the time the bad weather set in, he'd trained enough people to replace the bastards. He paid them half of what he'd been paying before. So who's stupid, I ask you?"

David is not sure he is supposed to answer, but he does anyway and guesses it must be those air traffic controllers who were stupid, not Reagan. By now he can tell this story is not meant to calm him down. It is simply something this man wishes to say, something he can't really say without another person to say it to. David wonders if he will ever want to tell stories to strangers. He tells himself that his father is a storyteller, that words are supposed to be a part of who he is, but he can't remember his father telling *him* any stories.

A flight attendant asks them what they would like to drink. David asks for another ginger ale. He knows he won't remember the story he has just been told. What he will retain is a picture of men in a high tower holding other men by their testicles.

⌗

Melvyn's is a cocktail lounge and restaurant in Palm Springs. It is exactly what David's mother has imagined a cocktail lounge in Palm Springs to look like: a place Frank Sinatra would frequent, a place with a long bar and high ceiling, a black grand piano, low lighting and pink walls. And now that she is here, she is disappointed. She is disappointed a city of such reputation could not exceed her imagination.

"Caroline," her fiancé says. He pronounces her name as though he is saying "airline" and sometimes breaks into an off-key version of a Neil Diamond song of the same name. They are sitting outside at a table looking across a thin veneer of lawn to a swimming pool and have just received their menus.

"What?" she says.

"Pumpkin soup," he says, reaching across and pointing to her menu.

"Yes andy?" she asks.

"Can you imagine anything weirder?" he asks.

His question consoles her. After her marriage to Peter, she is happy to see a man struck speechless by an appetizer.

"I want a big salad," she tells him. "Everywhere David and I went in Europe, they had these big salads." It's been a week. She's done her best to mention her son the way an ordinary mother might after a few days of separation. She hasn't tried to phone him, only sent a few postcards.

Caroline looks across at Andy now, making jokes with a busboy about the old folks bobbing around Melvyn's dance floor. This is what she likes about him, his refusal to take anything seriously. How long will she continue to compare Andy to Peter?

Children are our only hope of a love that doesn't recall anything but itself, she decides.

The next morning they eat breakfast at Sherman's, a kosher deli that will serve half a head of steamed cabbage if that's what you want. Andy and Caroline order bagels. She tells Andy she wants to see David. "You will," he says.

# ⌗

"Why are you doing that?" David asks his father. They are standing in a kitchen/living room/study. With a clear plastic hose, Peter is sucking wine out of a five-gallon glass carboy that sits on top of a wooden stool. A thin red snake of wine loops its way toward him. When it almost reaches his mouth, he pinches hard and inserts it into one of several smaller jugs at his feet.

"Why do you think?" Peter asks.

"I don't know," David says. Blackberry wine flows from one jar into the other when Peter releases his grip. A heady smell of fermented berries soaks the air.

"Which would *you* rather carry?" Peter asks. He gestures with both hands, one up, one down.

"Oh, yeah," David says.

"And, anyway, wine tastes funny if it sits on its sediment too long."

"It tastes funny no matter what you do to it," David says.

"How would you know?"

David shrugs his shoulders, as though he might take out a cigarette and light it, he's that bored. "I was in France, you know. Kids can drink there."

"Some kids, yeah, but who were you with?" Peter asks.

"She says it's good for me. She says I won't think it's such a big deal when I get older."

Peter screws an air lock into place and starts filling a second jug. "What she means," he says, "is you won't turn into an asshole like your father."

"She never said that," David says.

Peter wonders how much this boy carries in his head. What does he remember? But what we remember isn't always what's bothering us. *Hey, kid,* he wants to say. *Tell me what I owe.* Wine spews from the end of the hose. It pools and foams in the bottle, a tide on the rise.

The time with the rowboat…Peter fell in. Oars went flying. He lost his sandwich. When he broke the surface gasping from the cold and sucking in air, he told David he'd felt like a swim. They'd been out checking a crab trap. Rogue patches of morning fog drifted by. He knew he was in trouble. He couldn't risk boarding over gunwale or transom, so he swam to shore to get another boat, but not before he tied a line to the crab buoy. David wasn't going anywhere. Peter told him to pretend he was a singing foghorn. David sang "Skinnamarink-a-dinky-dink, skinnamarinky-doo." A fisherman heard David and picked him up before Peter had been gone 10 minutes. David was singing, "I love you" at the top of his lungs.

David watches his father fill another three jars. Peter tells him this wine has been commissioned by Bill Spears for his annual pig roast tomorrow night. David is astonished, not because he will see a whole pig skewered on a shaft of steel, but because this man crouching beside a growing forest of squat green bottles, watching a level line of dark clear liquid climb a wall of wavy transparent glass, is his father. It is as though he has been given this information for the first time, as though he has been an orphan all his life and has just been introduced. His eyes cannot open wide enough.

Since he arrived, he has been sleeping on a cot jammed in between two tall bookcases. Now David looks at those dust-covered shelves that hold volumes of poetry, biographies, essays on writing, collections of letters sent from one writer to another. Some of these books, he knows, were written by his father. He has never thought of reading his father's poetry, but now he searches row after row of spines for his father's name.

Andy and Caroline are now husband and wife. Andy wants to celebrate by getting up early and taking the shuttle bus into Disneyland, but Caroline says no. She could never do that, she says, without taking David too.

"But he's not here," Andy says.

"That's the point," Caroline says and once again wonders whether she has done the right thing. What else is *not* obvious to this man?

Andy settles for an hour-long spin in a dune buggy. Caroline sits beside him, strapped into her seat. She is in charge of the video camera. Sometimes she turns the camera on Andy. He grins broadly behind the visor on his helmet. He takes one hand off the wheel to wave and to yell that he loves her. They are driving straight into the sun.

Bill Spears invites all the islanders to his pig roast. Usually this means 150 people, sometimes more. It's potluck. It's BYOB. It's 10 acres of land that slopes east toward Mount Baker and the Strait of Georgia. A lame horse stands in a corral, poking his nose through a fence for carrots. Ducks swim under a bridge that straddles a homemade pond. Musicians settle in chairs and unpack mandolins, guitars, violins, dulcimers. Bill's wife shows newcomers through their log home, tells them how Bill wanted to *find* a banister, not *make* one. Everyone admires their stove.

Outside, men sign up to play bocci. Kids run in circles stealing pop, chips, cider, or beer. Kent Isbister has lit up Bill's porch with Fern Island Candles. He describes his process to people who ask, tells them how he lived on Maui for six months. He compares Hawaiian flora with local varieties, demonstrates how local sand is inferior to what he is used to. Granite makes for a coarser texture than white silicate, he tells them. Listeners nod, take his card.

Peter and David follow a trail that leads down a hill from Peter's shack. They emerge from a grove of trees. Each is carrying two jugs of wine, which they place on a table that will serve as a bar. Then they join a few people who have gathered to watch a pig rotate above a neon bed of coals. An electric motor from Bill's defunct washing machine turns a sprocket that moves a bicycle chain connected to a propeller shaft salvaged from a beached trawler. Transfixed through both anus and mouth, a pig that had spent his days fattening himself for this very occasion stares straight ahead, as though in death, as in life, he is performing his duty. Barbed wire lashes his legs to his body so that, every turn or so, drops of fat burst into flame. A girl on a cordless phone is giving advice to a friend. Her back is turned; she faces a wall of honeysuckle. "You always let this happen," she is saying. "She has no right to fuck you around this way."

Two boys challenge Peter and David to a game of bocci. They tell Peter it's two dollars a head to play, but the entry fee gives them a chance at $100. Each boy's underwear sits at least two inches above his belt. In another time, they would have looked like victims of a practical joke. While they are waiting to play, David tells them about Paris, about the skaters, how it's okay to skate even in public squares and around Notre Dame. The two boys tell David one of their friends has built a half-pipe in his yard, offer to lend him a skateboard since he left his at home.

One boy slips David a bottle of beer he has liberated from a barrel of cans and bottles and ice. They pass it around.

Just before dark, someone announces dinner. Candles and kerosene lamps line tables filled with salads, buns, pickles and corn. In his rush, a drunken boy runs directly into the stomach of a drunken man. "I'll be wreaking the havoc around here," the man tells the boy before he lets him go.

Shouts come from a small field, where people sit in lawn chairs or lie on blankets, drinking from bottles and watching a heated bocci tournament. They are watching Peter and David, who stand in the flickering light cast by five or six tiki torches arranged in a large circle. Two boys on the other side of the circle shout names and taunt. "Old man," one boy yells. "You are so old, old man."

David moves toward his father. They stand close together now, as though seeking protection from rain or wind. David hands him a green ball and, as Peter lofts a shot into wavering obscurity, David follows it with his eyes. "Good one," he says. "Good one."

# YELLOW WITH BLACK HORNS

**E**velina is drawing hearts of all sizes. Her stick carves a fine channel, pushing lumps of wet sand to either side. When the stick breaks in her hand, she crosses her arms and shakes her head, turns to a Chinese family digging clams about 20 yards away. *I have to leave you for a minute,* she says. *My chalk has broken.* The Chinese family continues to dig.

Evelina walks toward the driftwood that sits just above the high-tide line, her arms swinging like those of a soldier. From a pile of bleached slivers of cedar and fir, she chooses a replacement and returns. She finishes the largest heart and stands inside it. The wind coming in off the water lifts her hair off her shoulders and across her face.

*Yes,* she says. *That's very good.* She draws a lady with long hair. *What else can we put in our hearts?* She points her stick at a hotel in the distance. She draws a man with a hat and a moustache. *Today I will draw my brother too, because next week is his birthday.* She draws a boy and beside the boy she draws a cat, but by the time she has finished the ocean is tugging at her heels. Evelina does not understand the tides. She thinks the water is trying to trick her. Her father explained to her once about the moon, but there is no moon in the sky today. Evelina hates the way, piece by piece, the sea eats her hearts. She gathers up her socks and shoes and moves away from the water.

Her whole family is at the beach today, but not for the party. That's not until next week, in the backyard. She draws another heart and steps inside it. She draws the apple tree and then the piñata.

"Evelina! Time to go!"

Across the flat, grey stretch of sand, Evelina can see her mother picking up the blanket and shaking it. She lifts the tartan square so that it floats on the wind and when it begins to fall she gives it a good snap. Once, twice, three times. Each time she does it, the sound of the blanket's snapping reaches Evelina like an echo. Her father has left the beach ahead of everybody else. He is already walking toward the path, through the swordgrass and spindly young alders, to the parking lot. Evelina's brother, Peter, is tugging at his father's arm and crying. He would stay all day if his parents let him. Evelina extends her left arm behind her, imagining the weight of her brother pulling, digging his feet into the sand. She watches her father's steady steps. When her brother trips over a piece of wood, her father keeps moving, dragging Peter until he finds his feet again. She runs across the sand toward her mother, who has just finished closing the lid on the picnic basket. On her way, Evelina detours through some of the shallow, sun-warmed pools. Each time her feet enter the tepid water, she wants to sit down and cover her legs, cold now from the wind, but she can see her mother's hands struggling with the leather straps on the basket, so she keeps on running.

"How is it there's always more to take home than we brought?" her mother asks as Evelina comes up the beach toward her.

Evelina smiles, but her mother doesn't look at her. Her face is turned toward the path and the hole in the line of trees where

Peter and his father are disappearing from view. Evelina sits down on a log and brushes the sand from her feet before she puts on her runners. When she finishes, she picks up the folded blanket and follows her mother to the car. Evelina drops her stick in order to carry the blanket properly. As she lets it fall, something pulls at it. *Maybe it's the moon,* she thinks.

By the time they reach the parking lot, Peter is no longer crying. He is making faces at them through the rear window of the blue Pontiac. Evelina's father already has the engine running. His window is rolled down and he is tapping his fingers on the rim of the steering wheel, keeping time to the radio. The watery tune drifts out into the air along with the smoke from his cigarette. Evelina's mother lifts the trunk lid and puts in the picnic basket and the blanket. As she opens the door of the car to join her brother, Evelina feels her mother's hands on her shoulders and the gentle pressure of her face as her mother buries her nose in Evelina's hair. "You smell good," she says.

On the way home, Evelina thinks about the party. *I am six,* she reminds herself. *Peter is excited, because he will be four. I am older. I can wait.* She thinks about the apple tree in their backyard and her brother's friends. Tomorrow she and her mother are going to make the piñata while her father takes Peter out to their grandmother's. Nobody speaks as they drive home. Nobody except Peter, who is talking to the shells he clutches in either hand.

"Shut up, you," one shell says.

"I'll getcha," says the other.

They fight.

Sometimes late at night, after the family has been out visiting or to a movie, Evelina will see her mother slide across the front seat of the car to lean her head on her father's shoulder. And then her father will lift his arm and pull her in tight beside him.

Evelina loves his arm, his big arm. She likes to fall asleep watching their shapes blur in the glow of passing headlights.

But today her mother sits with one hand on the armrest, her eyes fixed on the forest beside the highway. Maybe she is looking for deer or raccoons. For a few minutes, Evelina watches for deer with her mother, but she soon gives up and starts to draw hearts on the mohair seat cover.

The next morning, Evelina doesn't bother her mother about the piñata. The phone rings at breakfast, but when her father answers it nobody is there. After he sits down at the table, it rings again, but still there is nobody on the other end. Her father says hello a few times. "What's the matter?" he says into the receiver. "Cat got your tongue?"

"Cat got your tongue, monkey got your bum!" yells Peter. He yells it again and again from his seat at the "special table." Peter is not big enough to sit in a normal chair like everybody else, but he refuses to use a booster seat.

"Pervert," Evelina's father says calmly into the phone, hanging it up with a firm clunk. He picks up a piece of toast from his plate and eats it standing up. He stuffs the final corner into his mouth and plucks Peter from his chair.

"Peter," he says. "Oh, Peter, Peter, nothing sweeter." He twirls Peter above his head like an airplane and plunks him back down. "Will *somebody* get this child ready so I can get to work on time? Not everyone gets the summer off, you know."

"Just call me 'somebody,'" Evelina's mother says.

"What did I say?" Evelina's father asks, grinning broadly. "Did I say something, Evelina?"

Evelina doesn't know what to answer. She looks at her mother, but her mother only shakes her head and takes a cloth to Peter's mucky face. Evelina goes back to her room to play with her dolls. From there she can listen through the heat vent to her family in the kitchen below. She can tell when it's not a good time to go downstairs. Peter hasn't learned this yet, not to be a nuisance. Evelina can hear him as he follows his father around the house asking him where they are going. She can hear her mother rummaging through the shoe drawer and the worn brass hinges as her father struggles with the back door. "Fine, then," he says after a few minutes. "Off with you, Peter."

Evelina can pick out her brother's small feet on the back porch. She recognizes the heavy footsteps of her father following Peter. Her father forgets to close the door behind him, but today her mother doesn't say a thing. As far as Evelina knows, Peter doesn't even have his shoes or coat on, but they go out anyway. Evelina waits a minute and then goes downstairs to find her mother in the living room watching the car back out of the driveway. When her mother turns around, she is biting her lip and her eyes are looking far away like the time she let the doctor take Peter to stitch up a nasty cut in his thumb. For a moment, Evelina thinks she should say something, but then the look on her mother's face changes. "Oh, you," she says. "Would you like to make the piñata now?" Evelina is glad she didn't have to ask.

In the kitchen, her mother pulls out a pile of newspapers from under the sink and shows Evelina how to tear them into strips. The two of them sit on the kitchen floor tearing newspaper and placing the strips into a pile. Evelina's mother mixes flour and water together in the bucket they use for washing the car and when the paste looks like pancake batter she picks up the bucket and tells Evelina to follow her down into the basement.

The basement is dark, lit only by two bulbs with pull chains. Evelina doesn't like to go down there, even during the day. The lights can't be turned on from upstairs. Every time her mother asks her to get a jar of pears from the preserve closet, Evelina wishes she could use the flashlight her father keeps in his top drawer. At night she loses her way and circles the floor, groping in the black air above her head for the chain. Today, in the dull light of the basement's only window, her mother finds the pull chains quickly.

Evelina's mother sets down the bucket of paste and goes to a large standing cupboard beside the washing machine. From the very back of the top shelf, she pulls something out. At first Evelina doesn't know what it is, but when her mother spins it around on the string tied to its middle, she sees it is a bull, shaped from the rusty chicken wire they used one year to keep cats out of the garden. Nothing much ever grew in their garden so her father turned the small black square of dirt into more lawn. He rolled up the chicken wire and shoved it behind the tool shed. What surprises Evelina is her mother. When did she go out to the shed and retrieve the wire? How could she have made such a thing without anyone knowing?

The bull isn't large, but it has horns like a real one. Her mother sets it down on the cement floor and shows Evelina the hole in the top where they will hide the prizes they bought last week in Chinatown and how the stomach of the bull is hinged so it will break open and let them fall out.

Evelina's mother starts dipping the strips of newspaper into the bucket of paste. When they're covered, she takes them one at a time and wraps them around a part of the wire frame. She covers the legs first, showing Evelina how to overlap the strips. "This way it will be strong," her mother says. "The boys will have to work hard to get their prizes."

She tells Evelina again of the time when she, too, was a little girl and broke her arm after a fall from the maple tree outside her window. Evelina likes to think of her mother running and climbing trees and bossing her sisters around. Evelina listens again to how the neighbour drove her mother and her grandmother to the hospital and how the doctor fixed her arm by placing it in a cast. "Today you and I are the doctors," she says. "We're making this bull strong the way Dr. Whitely made my arm strong."

Evelina imagines one of her own arms sheathed in layers of cloth soaked in plaster, cool, soothing, covering her wrist, her forearm and her elbow inch by inch and freezing them into a hard white *L*. She looks at the bull taking shape in front of her, its wire skeleton and paper skin. She thinks of the bull finished, the prizes tucked safely inside the dark cavity of its stomach. The paste drips from their hands onto the floor. Evelina wipes her forehead and leaves a wide streak of white in her hair.

"What was I thinking?" says her mother. "Take off your blouse and skirt. Socks and shoes too."

Evelina strips off her clothes and after hanging the bull from a wooden beam above the big laundry tubs, her mother strips down as well. They climb up and sit facing each other on the outer rims of the twin tubs, the bucket of paste balanced between them and their thighs pressing into the smooth cement edges of the old basins.

"Now we can make as much mess as we want," her mother says, starting in on the bull's shoulders and neck. Sun filters through the dusty curtains of the window above them. The bull hangs half-made on the string while Evelina's mother smoothes the dirty white skin that seems to grow out of her fingers.

⌗

In Chinatown the week before, Evelina and her mother looked in store after store for toys and candy to fill the piñata. They walked past groceries that spilled out onto the sidewalk with boxes of vegetables and fruit. Roast ducks turned on spits in windows and swirling neon letters lit up ceilings and restaurant arches. Men in dark suits stood in clumps, smoking and talking loudly. In one of the stores, rooms opened into more rooms and everywhere tables were piled high with brightly-painted trinkets. Evelina walked around, losing her mother and then finding her again. When they had seen everything, they left through a back door and ended up in a long, thin alley with open doorways that revealed steep staircases disappearing into the darkness. They stopped for lunch at a café with polished wooden booths and shared a plate of fried rice. Evelina drank pop; her mother drank Chinese tea. Evelina hoped that the waiter thought she and her mother looked like the sort of people who belonged in Chinatown, that he was treating them the same way he would treat a Chinese person.

"I'm sorry you don't have a sister," her mother said as they left the café. "Sisters are so much fun. We could pretend, if you want. Would you like that? Would you like it if I pretended I was your sister?"

"No," Evelina said.

"Why not?" her mother asked. "I think we'd be wonderful sisters. We could live in an apartment together and have tea parties for our friends."

"What about Peter," Evelina asked, "and Dad?"

"They could have an apartment too," her mother said. "We'd let them come and visit us."

"No," said Evelina. She didn't like this game. Her mother was playing it too seriously, as though Evelina's answers really mattered. As though they could really do such a thing, if only Evelina would say yes.

"Oh, Evelina," her mother said. "Don't you think it would be fun?"

"Yes," Evelina said, "but who would be our mother?"

⌗

Evelina doesn't know they are finished until her mother says they are. Instead of taking a bath, Evelina stays in the deep cement tub while her mother fills it with warm water. She is still small enough that if she crouches the water comes right up to her shoulders. The cold cement sides are an inch thick, but they get warm quickly as the water pours in. When Evelina closes her eyes, she feels as though she is sitting on the rough bottom of the wading pool at the park. She can almost hear the children splashing around her and see the other mothers stretched out on towels, talking and smoking. Evelina blinks and sees her mother, and then the bull, still wet above her, drying quickly in the muted sunlight.

The phone rings while they are dressing and Evelina's mother runs upstairs to answer it. Evelina listens and in a second she hears her mother talking. This time it's not a pervert. Her mother's voice is quiet and soft. It drifts down the basement stairwell and makes Evelina think of walking on the lawn. She towels herself dry and dresses quickly, but her mother has already hung up by the time Evelina joins her in the kitchen. "Who was that?" Evelina asks.

Her mother opens the fridge. "Are you hungry?" she asks. "Should we have some lunch now?"

The phone rings again and Evelina's mother turns from the refrigerator. "What a bother," she says. "Let's not answer it. Let's pretend we're not home. I'll make us some sandwiches and we'll have a picnic in the backyard." The phone continues to ring as her mother pulls a new jar of mayonnaise from the cupboard, a tomato and some lettuce from the crisper. "You find a blanket and spread it on the grass," she says. Evelina runs to the linen closet. With each insistent ring, she searches more frantically for a blanket. The ringing follows her out the back door and down the steps. When it refuses to stop, Evelina is almost ready to cry. She wants her mother to do something, to pick the phone up and scream at the person. Evelina is angry enough to do it herself. In another minute, she'll go into the house and tell that person to stop it, just to stop it, but then the sound is gone. A few minutes later, Evelina's mother steps out onto the back porch with a tray of sandwiches and a pitcher of Kool-Aid.

The air is warm in the backyard and when they have finished eating Evelina's mother brings the piñata out into the sun. It's Evelina's job to choose the paints. Evelina has never seen a bull, apart from the one in the stars her father showed her. *Each star a sun,* he told her, *just like ours.* "Yellow," she tells her mother, "with black horns."

When they've finished, Evelina paints a bright red heart on the bull's chest and then the two of them carry the piñata into the basement, where they hang it from a wooden beam in the darkness of the coal bin.

In the evening, Peter and his father return from their visit to grandma's. Peter carries a peach pie his grandmother has sent along. He places it proudly on the kitchen counter. "Tea party tonight," he says.

Peter is too young to care about Evelina's day, to wonder what Evelina was doing while he was at their grandmother's. Nevertheless, when he asks Evelina to help him build a fort under his bed, she is so relieved not to have to lie that she plays with him much longer than usual. There are still several days to go, but Evelina can see her brother doesn't suspect a thing.

Before bed, the family gathers for tea and pie in the living room. Evelina's father cuts four big pieces and passes them around. "Where did you go today?" he asks her mother.

"Nowhere," her mother says. "Evelina and I had a picnic in the backyard."

"Because I phoned a couple of times and there was no answer, that's all," he says.

"We didn't want to answer it because we thought it might be that pervert calling again. He called this morning after you left, you know."

"What did he say?" her father asks.

"Nothing," her mother says. "Not a thing."

&#9839;

Evelina visits the bull many times before the weekend. She doesn't even mind hunting for the pull chains. She doesn't take the piñata down, just stands outside the coal bin looking up into its black reaches, where she can barely make out the form of the bull turning on its string in the breeze she's brought with her. She tries to picture her brother seeing the piñata for the first time. *Will he really be surprised?* she wonders. *Will he think it's magic?* One day she pretends that she doesn't know the bull is there, that she has come upon it while looking for something else. In the living room above her head, her mother is lecturing Peter. "Don't stick your lip out at me," she is saying. Evelina, frightened, jumps back from the entrance to the coal bin. She thinks the bull has spoken to her.

&#9839;

On Saturday morning, Evelina wakes to the sound of the car backing out the driveway below her window. Her father's head craning to look behind him and the chrome of the Pontiac's grille are all she sees. In the kitchen, she finds her mother wiping up a spill on the floor. She's pulled her nightgown up past her knees and cinched it into a knot at her waist. Evelina watches from behind as her mother pushes a cloth back and forth over the bright red squares of linoleum tile, sopping up a pool of black coffee and squeezing it out into a dirty saucepan. A quarter to eight and Peter isn't even awake yet. His birthday isn't really until Monday, but Evelina still can't imagine how he can sleep so late. She moves to the table and sits down, waiting for her mother to notice her. In the top of the garbage bucket, she sees some shards of pottery, the crescent curve of a cup handle.

"Which one broke?" she asks.

"Oh, precious," her mother says, pulling herself around. "The Donald and Mickey." She hugs her knees and looks at Evelina. "I'm so sorry."

*Why would anyone use that mug when they knew it was mine?* Evelina thinks.

Her mother gets up and pours Evelina a glass of juice and fixes her some toast. "Evelina," she says, "I need you to be a big girl today." Evelina waits. "I won't have the car like I thought I would, so now someone will have to stay home with Peter while I walk to the store. Can you do that for me?"

Evelina isn't surprised by the request. When she hears the words come from her mother's mouth, she almost expects them. What startles Evelina, though, are the deep valleys of bloodless skin that have appeared between her mother's knuckles, the lines of taut muscle running down her neck.

Her mother unknots the nightgown bunched at her side and moves toward the hall. "If I leave now, I'll be back before the kids get here. Give Peter some cereal when he gets up. Don't fiddle with the toaster, okay?" More instructions trail down the stairs and over the banister. In the time it takes Evelina to finish her breakfast, her mother dresses, puts on some mascara and a little lipstick, checks the elements on the gas stove twice and leaves, locking the door behind her. Evelina hears her mother descend the front steps, the slap of her shoes on the cement walk. She listens until the footsteps fade completely and she is alone. She gets up and walks over to the garbage bucket to look at the pieces of her broken cup. She puts her fingers through the handle, removes them, then folds the top edges of the garbage bag over so the pieces are hidden. A lawn mower ignites the air somewhere down the street. Two cats screech at one another. Upstairs, Peter leaps from his bed onto the floor and yells for Evelina's mother to bring him his favourite shirt. At the same time, the phone rings, but Evelina ignores it and runs upstairs.

⌗

The birthday party is to start at 1:00 p.m. and Evelina's mother returns home at 11:30. She comes in through the back door, followed by a man carrying four large bags of groceries. He places them on the kitchen table and leaves, accepting the change Evelina's mother offers as he goes. Evelina watches quietly as her mother sits down to pull off her shoes and light a cigarette. Peter is in the living room with his bag of green army men. He has boxed together a cave from all the cushions on the sofa and the muffled sounds of his war games filter through to the kitchen.

Evelina's mother holds out an arm. "Come here, beauty," she says.

Evelina allows herself to fold into her mother's lap, her head tucked under her mother's chin. The smell of cigarette smoke on her mother's clothes is not unfamiliar, but it is rare, something reserved for late evenings and guests.

"We have lots of time," her mother says. "Lots of time."

The sun is high and the sky cloudless. Evelina and Peter trail coloured streamers around the backyard and unfold lawn chairs while their mother prepares party favours and ices a store-bought white cake. With her icing kit, she writes *Happy Birthday Peter* in red across the top and places four candles strategically around the letters.

A neatly dressed boy from two streets over rings the doorbell at precisely one o'clock, gift in hand. His parents wave from the sidewalk as he enters. "Four-thirty?" they ask as Evelina's mother waves back.

"Four-thirty," she says.

Other boys are already coming up the walk. Peter takes each boy's present and runs to the dining room, where he places it beside other presents on the table. Outside, several boys have already attacked the swing set. One boy is in the apple tree yelling down at the others to come after him. Evelina tries to show another how to use a badminton racquet. She throws the bird to the boy and after it lands on the ground the boy swings.

Evelina's mother appears on the porch and claps three times. "Line up for games," she says and the boys scramble to be first, as Evelina knew they would.

There are enough boys for a good game of pig-in-the-middle, but not quite enough for an egg-and-spoon race. Evelina is "it" in hide-and-seek, but Geoffrey, whose own birthday party is next weekend, gets scared and starts crying when Evelina jumps out at them. Her mother balances a penny on the top of a pile of flour and gives each of the boys a teaspoon. Each boy removes a spoonful of flour and the one who makes the penny fall has to run around the house.

Just before they stop for hot dogs, Evelina sits the boys on the grass under the apple tree and makes them close their eyes. She gives each boy a piece of paper, a pencil and a book to use as a drawing table. "Draw a cat," she says, "and no peeking." Evelina learned this game from her grade one teacher and often plays it on her own. The boys draw carefully with pencils tightly clenched between their fingers and tongues pinched between their lips. When Evelina tells them to stop and open their eyes, they look upon their work in silence. Cross-legged and confused, they stare up at Evelina. A trick has been played on them, but they are not sure what it is.

Hot dogs are brought out in a pot of boiling water and served with mustard and ketchup on white buns. Peter tells his mother he is going to eat four. "Save room for cake," she tells him.

Evelina knows it is time for the piñata, but she doesn't want to start without her father. He will want to watch Peter try to get the prizes. She has already asked her mother once when he will arrive. Reluctantly, Evelina disappears into the basement. From the beam in the coal bin, she unhooks the piñata and carries it out into the bright sunlight. All the boys turn in her direction as she appears, their mouths still full of wiener and bread.

"Surprise!" Evelina shouts. She explains to Peter and the others what her mother has told her, that in Mexico the children have birthday parties too but that at their parties they have piñatas full of prizes for everybody.

"You will have to work hard," she tells them and describes how they are to get the prizes out of the bull. The boys rush to line up and because it's Peter's birthday he gets to go first. Evelina ties a blindfold around his head and hands him a heavy wooden stick. Then she spins him in a circle and sends him off in the direction of the piñata. "You can have three tries," she tells him.

Peter's first swing sends him off balance and he falls to the ground. Evelina helps him up. His next two swings miss widely. Evelina is disappointed for him, but she also worries about what will happen to the thin plaster shell of the bull's body when one of the boys actually hits it. A boy called Stephen takes his turn next, but he, too, strikes only the air. Others follow, even farther from the mark. Evelina decides to stop spinning them before she sends them off and she allows them four tries instead of three. One boy nicks the leg of the bull and sends it careening from side to side.

"Can I have a hit?" Evelina's father comes through the gate into the backyard. He walks up to the line of boys and stands waiting. His jacket is unbuttoned and a tie hangs out of the left pocket, where it has been stuffed in haste.

"It's the piñata," Evelina says. "For Peter's birthday."

"I'm a boy," her father says. "I want to play too."

Evelina is silent.

"Come on, sweetheart," her father says. "Cover my eyes." He kneels down on the grass and closes them.

Evelina's mother is sitting in a white metal chair under the clematis that hangs from the porch. She is holding a cup of coffee and smiling thinly at Evelina. Evelina takes the handkerchief and covers her father's eyes, tying it in a loose knot at the back of his head. His hair is stiff with grease. She hands him the stick.

"Spin me, Evelina," her father says, standing.

Evelina places her hands on her father's waist and turns. She might as well be trying to twist a fir tree. Her father's body passes beneath her hands as he completes a circle and stops.

"Okay," her father says. He strides toward the apple tree and raises the stick. The back of the bull is broken from the force of her father's blow, crushed inward to reveal the web of rusty chicken wire that holds the bull together.

Evelina turns to her mother sitting in the white chair, her cup of coffee lying empty on the grass. She is pointing at Evelina's blindfolded father, trying to say something, but short bursts of laughter like hiccups keep interrupting her words. "A little late for that," she says. "Aren't you just a little too late?"

Evelina turns back in time to see her father taking up the stick again for a second blow. He stands as though he is at bat in a baseball game, his arms drawn back ready to swing. This time he hits the bull full in the stomach. The wire hinges break and a yawning gap appears in the underbelly, spilling popguns, Chinese yo-yos and magic rings onto the grass below.

Peter and the others move in to scoop up the treasure, grabbing as many prizes as they can hold.

Evelina's father pulls off the blindfold and leans on the stick. "There you go, boys," he says. "That's how it's done."

Evelina imagined the piñata would crack slowly, like the shell of an egg when a chick is born. She certainly didn't think her father would want to join in the game or that her mother would find it so funny when he did. *It's all wrong*, she thinks. *Everything is wrong*. She starts pulling the boys back from the pile of prizes. She rips the candies and cheap toys out of their pockets and slaps their hands to make them drop what they are holding. Peter runs by her, dodging, keeping himself low to the ground, responding quickly to this new development in the game. He is going back for more, but Evelina catches him by the scruff of his neck and hits him hard across the side of his face. She hits him again and then again until he cries. "Hey!" she hears her mother say. "Hey, now!"

# IN BED

**B**lake grabbed his flashlight from the shelf above the dryer, the caulking gun already tucked under one arm. His hands were protected by a pair of motorcycle gauntlets. He wore a plastic safety visor. He stepped out the door into a second of blackness before the motion detector kicked in and flooded the yard with light. *I look like a thief*, he thought.

On the dark side of the house, he scanned the shingles for signs of activity. Ridges of grey silicone caulking filled the spaces between shingles. Nothing moved. The wasps were asleep.

"Is that you, Dad?" Blake's daughter Alix coasted up the driveway, bumping open the swinging gate with her front tire.

"Sweetheart," Blake said. "How'd it go?" He pushed the nozzle of the caulking gun into a hole.

"We lost," Alix said. She was 13. She played soccer Friday nights and Saturday mornings for a *B* team in the local division. Soccer wasn't a big sport in Olympia, but since the World Cup it had grown in popularity.

"Those are the breaks," Blake said. He squeezed the pump handle and watched the bead of silicone flow into the hole. He could feel it spreading out into the spaces under the shingle. *Let them figure this one out*, he boasted.

"Is there anything to eat?" Alix asked.

"There's soup left," Blake said, dropping the gun to his side.

"Anything else?"

"You don't like the soup?"

"We've been eating it for a week," Alix said.

"Three days," said Blake. "Four if you count today."

"Whatever," Alix said. She leaned her bike against the trellis at the end of the driveway and uncoiled the cable lock wrapped around the seat. Blake shone the flashlight on the combination while Alix twisted numbers. She stamped her feet at the same time. Clumps of dirt and grass fell from her soccer cleats onto the cement, holes neatly punched through each clod. "If I had a key lock," said Alix.

"You'd lose the key," said Blake.

The light in the backyard clicked off and Alix jumped in front of it waving her arms. Triggered again, the beam caught her in midair: skinny, blonde, limbs pushing out in all directions. She was a pale moth, legs like antennae, fluttering. Blake saw it all. He imagined himself a photographer. *Hold it,* he thought.

Blake sealed a few more likely holes before he joined Alix in the kitchen. He flipped the handle of the deadbolt and felt the three-inch steel rod click into place. He had installed the lock himself.

"How're the wasps doing?" Alix said. She had her head in the fridge.

"Today they were dying to get in," said Blake. "Tomorrow they'll be dying to get out. I don't care as long as they're dying."

"What about poison?" asked Alix. "It'd be quicker." She pulled a bagel from the cupboard above the sink and began rummaging for a steak knife. A tub of cream cheese sat on the counter.

"Don't need it. Don't like it," said Blake. "You want to be careful with that."

"Ow!" said Alix.

"Run it under the tap. I'll get you a Band-Aid."

Blake worked at a government liquor store in downtown Olympia: local wines, some imported, gin, rye, all the hard stuff, liqueurs, no beer. His wife, Shauna, landed a job with communications in the state legislature two years ago, just after she and Blake had gotten back together. It didn't take long for them to decide to leave Seattle for good. Alix was in grade six then. Part of Blake believed leaving Seattle had to do with the time two teenagers tried to pull him off his motorcycle along the waterfront, by Pier 38. He lost his pack and the loaf of banana bread he'd agreed to take to Shauna's; it was the only dessert he knew how to make. He couldn't stop shaking, so Shauna ran him a bath. She told him he wasn't fit to drive. She asked him to stay the night. So ended the separation and two years later they had a view of the sound and bought free-range eggs from their neighbours, but Blake still liked the feel of a good lock.

"Mom phone?" asked Alix. Two pink strips crossed the knuckle on the little finger of her right hand. The skin around the cut pulsed an antiseptic orange.

"Not tonight," said Blake. He sat at the breakfast bar, the entertainment section of the *Post-Intelligencer* folded into a square. Blake always did the cryptic crossword.

Alix sat on the stool beside him, painting mercurochrome onto her only long nail. "You know what time it is there?"

"Masonry," said Blake, his pen poised.

"It's nearly midnight. I'd be in bed if I were there. Do you think she's in bed?"

"Mother and child featured in stonework. Get it? Ma-son-ry. It's beautiful."

"Three weeks is a long time, Dad."

"Sweet creature, don't I know it," said Blake.

⌗

South African sherry was moving fast. The first three cases had sold in a day and people were reserving two, sometimes three bottles from the next shipment. Blake tilted a stack of five cases of Black Velvet and slipped the dolly underneath it. He rolled the cases along the wooden bed of the freight truck and down the ramp onto the loading bay.

Lorne Nichols was right behind him. "Still batching it, Blake?" Lorne fished during the summers and made do with part-time work during the winters.

"I'm living with someone," said Blake. He headed into the warehouse.

Lorne followed him. "You're living with someone. Blake Winter who won't even grab an extra newspaper from the pay box has dumped his wife and is living with someone," said Lorne.

"She's 13, too," said Blake. He wheeled around and winked at Lorne.

"Right," said Lorne. "Okay."

After unloading, Blake washed his hands and joined the others for a break in the coffee room. Lorne was shaking some whitener into a mug. It said in big green letters, "You look like a million dollars." Judy was flipping through a copy of *Hustler*. Blake pulled yesterday's crossword from his back pocket, unfolded it and laid it on the table. Judy was a lifer. She'd been at the store longer than anyone else. Her husband, Rupert, was Alix's soccer coach. He worked for a private highways maintenance company that repaired potholes, fixed signs and picked up litter. Rupert spent a lot of his time collecting aluminum beer cans from the ditches and medians. He didn't turn them in for a refund; he ripped the tops and bottoms off, slit the cans down one side and flattened them. Rupert would be up to 20,000 soon.

"Who wants first lunch?" said Judy.

"I'll take it," said Blake.

"A little hungry, Blake?" said Lorne. "No home cooking?"

"Alix is playing over at Carnarvon. I can catch the last half." Blake arranged the letters of the words "a nether land" into an anagram circle.

"It's a sad thing to see a man reduced to lying," said Lorne.

"Lorne, please," said Blake.

"All I'm saying is there's no way I'd let any wife of mine run off to Chicago for a month, course or no course."

"You don't have a wife, Lorne," said Blake.

"Doesn't matter," said Lorne. "It's the principle." He straddled a chair backward, his hands planted on his knees.

"What principle?" asked Blake.

"All right. Common sense, then. How do you know what she's doing back there? You don't. There's no telling what's going on. Human nature, Blake. People forget themselves. They talk to someone. They meet them for coffee. I'm telling you, Blake, a man shouldn't let his guard down for a minute."

"How was fishing this summer, Lorne?" asked Blake. "Catch much?"

"Don't say I didn't warn you, that's all," said Lorne.

Judy closed the *Hustler* and looked up at Blake. "You're off at 11, then," she said. "Say 'hey' to Rupert for me."

Blake took his pencil and filled in the 11-letter word "neanderthal."

⌗

Alix was on the sidelines when Blake arrived at Carnarvon Park. She pawed the ground and hugged herself in the cool fall air. Rupert was standing halfway down the field with a yellow flag, pointing in the direction of Alix's goalie. Poplars bordered the pitch on all sides, four golden walls suggesting a room with no roof, a space, a safe and enduring enclosure that Blake found familiar. He had attended an eastern prep school for a few years on a scholarship. He had not been good at sports, but had played on the junior soccer team while his scholarship lasted. Blake liked the game, not for its reputation of fair play or lack of violence, but because players so quickly gave up the use of their hands. He liked the seriousness, even horror, they expressed when someone forgot and gave in to the temptation to grab or block.

Alix waved and ran over. "We're kicking their butt, Dad," she said.

"Creature," Blake said, "I'm so pleased." He drew her into his coat and sniffed her hair. For a second, he felt the urge to pick her up and carry her on his shoulders so she could see better. "What's Rupert got you doing today?" he asked.

"Midfield and forward," she said. "I scored too. I took it all the way to the 18-yard line and bounced one in off the bar. I wish you'd seen it. I was great."

"You *are* great, sweetheart," said Blake. "It looks like Rupert wants to put you in again."

Rupert was calling to the referee for a substitution and waving at Alix. He saw Blake, held out his fist and gave him the thumbs-up. Blake joined his hands together and shook them above his head. The referee blew the whistle.

Dog walkers passed behind the goal nets on their way across the park. Some stood and watched the game, leashes in hand while their dogs strained to explore. A police car pulled into the parking lot, turned a slow circle and left again. Blake followed Alix's green jersey as Alix stuck to her check, dogging her up the wing and intercepting passes headed his way. She was so familiar that Blake wondered if he ever really saw her at all.

At Cooperhouse Preparatory School, Blake had roomed with a Jewish boy whose father had been hospitalized after a house fire. From the moment he got the news until they sent his father home, the boy would not eat or sleep. Blake kept trying to tell him the doctors would save his father, but he wouldn't listen, only tore at the ends of his fingers, saying, "It's my father, for God's sake! It's my father." Blake thought of that boy now and it was as if someone had shown Blake a picture of something and had put it back in a wallet before he'd had time to figure out what it was. This was how he felt about Alix. There was something he wasn't getting.

It was nearing noon, the end of Blake's lunch. The last five minutes of the game were played in fog, a slow blurring, first of the buildings and cars beyond the perimeter of the trees, then of the trees themselves, and finally, one by one, of the players on the field who passed in front of Blake like startled fish in a deep ocean trench. Three short blasts from the referee signalled the end of the second half. Alix's team gathered into a huddle and gave three cheers, then walked past the opposing team single file, shaking hands.

"Practice at 6:30 next Tuesday," Rupert shouted as he walked away with the net of soccer balls over his shoulder.

"Judy says hello," Blake yelled in return, but Rupert had disappeared.

The sun was threatening to burn through the fog and the air hung bright and overexposed around the silhouettes remaining on the field. Alix appeared at Blake's side out of breath and laughing. "You're a goon, Dad," she said. "A real goon."

"I am?" asked Blake.

"Trust me," said Alix, slipping her arm through his.

They walked to the concession where Alix's bike slumped, tethered to a chain-link fence. The yellow cinder blocks of the small building were scarred with broad black scrawls: *Think again.* Heavy plywood shutters covered the service counters, multiple stainless steel padlocks securing them. Blake blew rings from his mouth into the fog.

"What do I get for winning?" asked Alix, clicking the ends of her bike lock together.

"Get?" asked Blake.

"A reward. A treat. A prize. You know."

"What do you want?"

"Guess," said Alix. She swung the cable loop around her arm like a hula-hoop.

"Your own filing cabinet," said Blake.

"Nope."

"Some new dish gloves?"

"Come on, Dad. You're not trying," said Alix.

"I give up," said Blake.

"Chinese," said Alix.

Alix biked to a friend's house and Blake returned to work. He spent most of the afternoon on cash. Faces funnelled by, some familiar, some new. He used to imagine their lives, even ask questions, when he first started. Now he just took their money and made change. A woman brought in a bottle of Paul Masson white. It had gone off, she said. The bottle was half empty. Blake gave her another one. Judy pulled Lorne off stock and put him to work fixing the automatic exit. It stuck halfway about every third time and people were banging their heads. At 4:30, Blake turned in his float and the day's take and punched out.

He drove north out of Olympia. The roads narrowed and twisted among hobby farms and older, established acreages, the smell of the sea strong at the southern end of Puget Sound. He drove for about two miles and turned up the rough cement driveway at the top of the small knoll covered with second-growth fir and arbutus. Their home had been built in the early 20s: wood frame, shingle siding, a sleeping porch facing the east. Cheap at Seattle prices and twice as large a lot. Blake entered by the rear door. No sign of Alix's bike. He had told Alix to stay at Jessica's until he got off work. He didn't like her coming home to an empty house. Blake ignored the mail. He even passed the blinking light on the answering machine. He did what he had done every day after work for the past few days: he went immediately to the outside wall in the dining room and kneeled down below the window to give the plaster a good hard thump. A low, angry hum telegraphed through the plaster and the layers of wallpaper, tickling the lobe of his ear.

The wasps were still alive.

Blake opened the sash and looked down at the shingles he'd caulked the past few nights. In the dying light of late afternoon, he watched for escapees, trailblazing wasps that could negotiate the labyrinth of two-by-fours and strapping, past the six tubes of silicone squeezed into every likely access and out into the open air. None appeared. *Victory,* thought Blake.

He knew it was crazy, this plotting. In the cool autumn weather, they would die soon anyway. They were already getting dopey and slow, unresponsive to idle swipes with a hand. But he liked to believe this daily frustration, their mass panic when they found themselves locked in, would be transmitted to other wasp populations, that those sealed in alive would act as a warning to the next interloper, the next opportunist that came knocking. He told himself this punishment made more of a bang in the insect cosmos than a quick snuffing out by poison. Blake told himself all kinds of things, but revenge was what he wanted.

*For the love of God,* he pretended the wasps were saying to him behind the wall. *For the love of God.*

Blake returned to the kitchen and pressed the play button on the answering machine. After a furious rewinding, he heard Alix asking him to pick her up on the way to town and to bring her new jeans (in the dryer), her Docs, Mom's Guatemalan pullover and her brush. She'd change at Jessica's. Oh, yes, he was most certainly a goon.

The second message was from Shauna. "Hi, you guys," she said. "It's Saturday, three o'clock. I'm working late tonight, so I thought I'd phone now just to make sure you knew what time the plane landed. It's at 2:20 tomorrow. That's PST, so don't be late. Sunday traffic shouldn't be bad, but leave in good time. I miss you. Bye."

He played it three times. Each time she said something different.

The house was quiet. Blake padded into the living room. SET CLOCK flashed insistently on the VCR. He'd forgotten to open the blinds this morning and the last moments of sun steeped the room in pale green. Outside, birds announced it would be night soon, charting their territory with song. Blake moved across the hall into the master bedroom.

*What if I was here to rob the place?* he thought. *What if I just broke in?*

Suddenly he couldn't bring himself to turn on the light. *This is how everything looks to the criminal mind,* Blake decided. He saw his life reduced to a clock radio, the row of antique silver bells below the mirror, his Harris rod and reel balanced against the armoire.

When Shauna fell in love with someone else, Blake packed what he could still find of his life and moved into a basement suite near Elliott Bay, a district with a few seedy taverns and cheap, low-income rentals. There were bars and shutters on everything. He got used to having no curtains. When he couldn't think of any reason to stay awake, he slept.

The key to their old place was still on his ring, so he went back in the middle of the day to grab a few records he knew Shauna would never play. He knocked, just in case, and then he went in. There was nothing to distinguish this time from all the other times. He could have taken off early from work and come home to make dinner. He called Shauna's name on the chance Shauna hadn't heard him knocking. He walked down the hall and into the living room. He thought he'd see a coat, maybe a chair he wouldn't recognize, some books, a strange brand of beer. He passed the room where their bed was. He saw nothing. He saw everything. He left the records with the others and tiptoed out.

Now in the bedroom of his own house, Blake felt like a stranger again. He approached Shauna's dresser. The drawer slid out easily. The pullover Alix wanted was on the top. He grabbed it roughly, forgetting to close the drawer, and made a beeline for the dryer and shoe bin. Then he fled.

"Other people might have dandruff," Alix said, "or lice." She pushed a few loose strands of hair behind her ears. Alix never used other people's hairbrushes.

"I was in a hurry," Blake said. "Your friends don't have lice, anyway." It was a bad moment. Blake couldn't bear failing Alix. He talked about the game and then about dinner and by the time they pulled into town she was whistling.

Blake parked across the street. They walked over to the restaurant, entered the red-and-gold foyer and took a place in line by a wall-sized fish tank. Five minutes and they were seated near a window, nonsmoking, a pot of tea between them and a menu each. Alix bit off split ends while Blake made suggestions.

"Forty-four sounds good," he said.

Alix shuffled her menu. "I don't like shrimp," she said.

"Give them to me. I'll eat them," Blake said.

"Keep talking," she said.

"How about a hot pot? Beef, chicken. Pork if you want."

"Too spicy."

The waiter came. Blake ordered corn chowder for two, chicken chow mein and beef chop suey. Alix wanted a Shirley Temple. Blake asked for white wine. Two men and a woman at the next table were talking loudly, an empty pitcher of beer and three glasses on the table.

"You're going to think I'm crazy," one of the men was saying, "but this is what I call a good time. Don't you think this is a good time? Look at what's going on here. When we think about what's good in our lives, what do we think about? Times like this. It's true. I know *I* do. Am I crazy, or what?"

"People are different," the woman said. "Not everyone thinks like you."

The soup arrived and Blake ladled their servings. Clouds of egg yolk hung suspended in the bowls, the steam sweet with the smell of canned corn. They ate in hungry silence, blowing across the ceramic spoons to cool each mouthful, burning their tongues in haste and gulping down ice water. Blake paused to look at the photographs on the walls: old black and whites of the early part of the century, families on picnics, taverns and men with long beards raising glasses of beer. Over the bar was a big picture of a woman in a long dress holding on to the tail of a cow and laughing.

"She looks like Mom," Alix said when Blake pointed it out.

"Her mouth," Blake said. He spooned the last of the two dishes onto Alix's plate. "Help me out, partner."

The waiter brought the bill on a plate with two fortune cookies. Blake reached for one, but Alix covered them with her hand. "No, wait," she said.

Blake waited.

"Jessica's parents always do this *thing* when they get their fortune cookies," Alix said.

"What do they do?" Blake asked.

"They always say the words *in bed* before they read out their fortune."

"Why do they do that?"

"You'll see," said Alix. She split open her cookie, extracted the slip of pink paper and read it aloud. "In bed, ingenuity is the source of your greatest delight."

"Jessica's parents do this?" Blake asked.

"Yes, now read yours," Alix said.

"I'm not sure I want to," said Blake, reaching for the plate.

"Don't be a prude, Dad. It's fun."

Blake unfolded his fortune. "In bed," he said, "to give happiness is to deserve happiness."

"See? I told you." Alix left her seat and picked up a few pink slips left behind by the people at the next table. "In bed, you have a fine capacity for the enjoyment of life."

A couple by the exit looked up from their meal. Blake filled out the VISA slip.

"In bed," Alix continued, "the greatest remedy for anger is delay."

"Okay, creature," said Blake. "Let's boogie."

"One more," said Alix.

Blake shrugged.

"In bed," said Alix, "hope for the best, but prepare for the worst."

⋕

Through the window, Blake watched clouds pass in front of the moon. Fall storms were moving in from the coast. Behind his head and on the other side of the wall, Alix slept under the eiderdown she'd received for her last birthday. Blake would let her sleep in late tomorrow. When she got up, he'd fix her some pancakes and around noon they'd head for the Seattle airport to meet Shauna. He thought of the journey up the interstate through Tacoma. He thought of Rupert collecting cans from the side of the road. He thought of the stoplight where those two kids had come out of nowhere and grabbed him from behind. How he'd slipped the clutch and twisted the throttle and how they'd hung on, laughing, not content until they had a piece of him. He thought of Shauna, how she would appear at the arrival gate tomorrow, her face rising out of the crowd without warning, looking for him and Alix, looking for two faces that were looking for her. Blake knew what it was like to look for Shauna. He could pick her out with nothing more than a glimpse of the back of her knee, a shoulder, the tip of an ear. On the verge of a dream, Blake remembered how he felt when he saw even that much. He tried to imagine what it was like for Shauna to look for him, if this time she'd be disappointed with what she saw.

# THE BERLIN WALL

**M**arilyn tells him right on the hall stairs that she is renting out her children's rooms. The yellow was Karen's and the blue was Daniel's. She doesn't tell him both children would probably be in their rooms this very minute, playing video games or reading comics, if her husband hadn't been such a stupid man and if she hadn't been an even stupider woman.

"I must share this room?" he asks.

Marilyn's eyes are level with his, but the prospective boarder stands two steps below her. His backpack is festooned with baggage tags and a hand-stitched German flag.

"My children aren't here right now," she says.

"They are still their rooms, of course. I understand this." He blinks twice and pushes his glasses higher up the bridge of his nose.

"You can use my daughter's for as long as you want," Marilyn says.

"Perhaps your children will want their rooms back one day?" he asks.

Marilyn turns and heads up to the second-floor landing. "Not if they have any brains," she says.

She opens the door to her daughter's room and steps aside to let the young German enter. The hinges protest slightly and, although she has been renting out these rooms for almost five months, she still nourishes hope that Karen will be waiting on the other side of the door. The room is pretty bare bones, but clean. The walls have been relieved of posters and only a couple of specimens from her daughter's collection of perfume bottles remain on the bureau. It is a bedroom, after all.

He takes off his pack and sits it upright on the bed. He is what she expects a German to look like. She finds it disappointing just to be in the same room with him. His hair is a dusty haystack. His glasses are round with thin wire frames. His passport says he is 17. "I like this room very much," he says.

Out in the garden, Mac is on his knees planting some thinnings a neighbour has given him: a dozen Swiss chard plants and six kale. The pale fronds of Swiss chard lie limp and unenthusiastic on the dark soil while Mac attends to the kale. Marilyn doesn't like greens of any kind. Neither does Mac. Most vegetables, for that matter. He gives the bulk of what he grows to friends or serves it to the boarders. Once in a while, he makes Marilyn drive him down to the food bank, where he leaves a sack of whatever is in season. Right now it is tomatoes and corn and beets.

Above him a window swings open and Mac sees a blond head peer out over the neighbours' backyards. The head scans the rooftops in a slow semicircle, stopping midway to take a glimpse of the sea, and then lowers to face the garden. When it sees Mac, an arm joins the head and waves. Mac raises his trowel in salute. "Okay," the head says. "All right, man."

Mac moved in with his niece Marilyn after his wife, Emily, died exactly a year ago this September 5th, not long after

Marilyn lost the kids. Mac is a retired small-engine mechanic: weed eaters, leaf blowers, rototillers. By the time he stopped working, he also knew everything there was to know about the snowmobile. His wife died in Paris, in a room on the top floor of the Hotel Garnier, near the train station. He brought her ashes home in a carry-on and scattered them in the bay not too far from Marilyn's house. Until Emily's death, Mac and his wife had spent two weeks every summer camped in the driveway of Marilyn and Evan's faded clapboard two storey in Newport, Oregon. It was as close to the sea as they could afford and, until the trip to France, the farthest they'd ever travelled from their home in Whitefish, Montana.

Mac's first attempt to fly home with his wife's ashes was a failure. Going through customs, Mac was stopped by an official who wanted to see the contents of the cardboard box he was carrying. The weight of the box disturbed the official, even though it did not register as metal on the scanner. When he discovered what the box contained, he refused Mac permission to board the plane. "The transportation of human remains," he said, "is a serious matter."

The funeral parlour had said nothing about airline policy, neither had the police. Mac returned to the same hotel and was given the same room. He had asked for a single, but none was available. He spent another five days in Paris, two longer than he and Emily had originally planned. He walked through the Bois-de-Boulogne again. He revisited la rue Mouffetard and got drunk at la Negre Joyeuse. He bought chestnuts from the man outside Notre Dame. By the time the documentation arrived permitting him to return home, he had begun to wonder what his hurry was.

Mac rented a boat for Emily's burial at sea. On the way back to the marina, the motor cut out and Mac had to take the cover off the outboard and adjust the mixture. When he told the rental people what he'd done, they offered him a job filling in on weekends. He pays Marilyn $200 a month to sleep in the den, the room at the front of the house Evan used to call his office. Evan sold dope. Mollycoddled, fertilizer-fed, house-bound marijuana raised under 30 grow lamps that cost a fortune in electricity. When the power authority decided to share the consumption rates of its customers with the state police, Evan went to jail. A drug squad stripped the attic of 90 healthy plants, an acre of tinfoil, three boxes of spent bulbs and 15 gallons of liquid nutrient. After they left, Child Services made a case for Karen and Daniel — phoned by a neighbour? the school? — and within a week they were gone, too. Marilyn got to keep the house.

"We should take in boarders," Mac suggested to Marilyn six months later. She had secured work cleaning offices after hours, but it clearly wasn't enough income. Her two-year college diploma in criminology was next to useless, though she was now qualified to work as a prison guard, an irony she refused to acknowledge.

Their tenants are usually tourists who have come to spend a few days, perhaps a few weeks, in this quiet town next to the ocean. Mac prepares the meals, keeps the bathrooms tolerable, washes up. Marilyn pins notices to telephone poles, takes calls. Summer fare is steady in Newport; word gets around. At night, from his hide-a-bed in the den, Mac can hear the low murmur of couples as they review their day, plan the next one. He hears doors open in the middle of the night as men and women haul themselves from their dreams to the bathroom. He hears their lovemaking too, a sound he has always liked for its ability to lull him into the deepest of sleeps.

Sometimes the boarders leave things: rocks they pick up on their strolls by the bay, brochures from the harbour hotels. Once, while he was cleaning under the bed in Karen's old room, he found a straight razor, the blade worn into a curve and the ivory handle yellow with age. The discovery puzzled him because the person who had just vacated the room was a woman. He put the razor into a box in the basement along with everything else he'd found. He usually tries to track down the owner if he thinks the article might be missed, but he's had no luck with the razor.

⌗

Marilyn sits in the kitchen reading over the letter from the local branch of the Rotary club. It came yesterday.

> *Dear Fo'c'sle Boarding House,*
>
> *The Newport Branch of the Harbourview Rotarians wishes to thank you for acting as host family for this year's exchange student, Dieter Lippa. We hope you will be able to attend the formal welcome dinner taking place Saturday, September 21st, at 7:00 p.m. in the Trav-L-Lodge.*
>
> *Sincerely,*
>
> *Peter Trippet*
>
> *Treasurer: Harbourview Rotarians, District 502*

Mac tells Marilyn the student is a gift horse. Winter traffic, he says, that's what they need. The Rotary people are a steady paycheque. Let them throw a little money her way. Mac makes everything sound so exciting. She places the letter in a cake tin with all the other mail. She pulls out the postcards she received from Karen and Daniel during their summer vacation. They went to Disneyland for two weeks with Marilyn's mother and father (into whose hands the state has seen fit to place them). Marilyn would have preferred the new guardians be total strangers. Her parents perform their roles as foster parents as though they are administering a regimen of therapeutic drugs. The dosage of visitations must be regulated and monitored constantly and they must always take place at their home in Eugene. Marilyn manages to bite her tongue most of the time.

The kids' postcards didn't arrive at Marilyn's house until the trip was over. Karen phoned to ask if she had received them.

"No," Marilyn told her, "not yet."

Daniel giggled on the extension. Marilyn pictured Karen in the kitchen of her parents' home and Daniel in the living room, but really she had no idea where they were. The two of them yelled through the earpiece at her in disbelief.

"Of course you have them, silly," Daniel said. "We mailed them to you."

Marilyn could think of nothing to say in return. Was this a test? Then her mother joined in on a third extension. "How's my baby brother?" she asked, yelling too. "Marilyn, how's Mac?"

Marilyn saw herself holding three long black strings, a gaping mouth at each end. She didn't want to listen, to hear her children talk about themselves as though they were distant relatives, to digest the chunks her mother had bitten out of their days for force feeding. She wanted to hang up without even wishing them goodbye. She lied instead, told them someone was at the door. *A strategical error,* she thought as she placed the receiver in its cradle. There'd be little chance now of their coming home for the start of the school year. When the postcards came the next day, she phoned to tell them, but her mother said they were outside playing.

Marilyn shuffles the correspondence as though it is a deck of cards. There's a postcard from the Conestoga Hotel. Karen wrote out the menu for room service and underlined her choices. *We went swimming in the rain,* she wrote at the bottom. Another one shows the Pirates of the Caribbean with a circle inked in and *We stood here* in tiny letters. From an envelope, Marilyn pulls out two framed silhouettes, one of Karen and another of Daniel. The letter that came with the silhouettes describes how the man who made them used nothing more than a pair of scissors. She recognizes their black outlines, can distinguish each one easily. There are a few letters from Evan mixed in with the children's mail, but she feels no urge to give them a second read. His high school scrawl hasn't changed in 20 years and she mocks the PWB at the bottom of his note. *Please write back.* It's as though he's been skipping class and this was smuggled out of detention hall. She returns the thin stack of cards and letters to the tin and closes the lid, disgusted with herself.

Marilyn looks out the window at Mac working in the garden. Before he came to stay, she used to walk out in the evenings to the floating fish-and-chip sit-in/take-out next to the boat rental at the marina. Cooking for one was an art that eluded her. She would sit in one of the white plastic chairs littered about the wharf and listen to the wooden hulls nudge up against their moorings, feel the deck rise and fall with the wakes of passing boats. Even when both rooms are taken and Mac has dinner on the table, she occasionally strolls down to the marina. "Taking the night off," as Mac calls it. She watches him press his fingers into the soil around the base of some green thing he is planting. He is a man, she gratefully realizes, who will take her to her grave if he has to.

⌗

Dieter Lippa wakes to his third morning in America. He showers and brushes his teeth and pees a bright red stream of pee: beets. He comes downstairs and drinks a cup of coffee with the old man who tells Dieter to call him Mac. Dieter then walks two blocks to Seaview High School.

"Hello," he says to a boy in long baggy shorts who balances

a skateboard at his side as though he's carrying a plank. "My name is Dieter. I am from Germany."

A girl and two other boys in shorts, also with skateboards, join them. "West or East?" the girl asks. She is wearing a full-length Indian skirt, a peasant blouse and steel-toed boots.

"We are unified now," Dieter says. "One country, just like you."

"Cool," the girl says.

"Yes, it is," Dieter says. "It is very cool."

The girl's name is Bree and her brother is Chris. They live in a house built by an inventor. It has eight sides and rotates. "When I want the sun in my room, I just flick a switch," Bree says. She snaps her fingers.

"What do you do if you both want the sun?" Dieter asks.

The morning scoots by. Dieter is given a timetable and a combination lock. He will be studying modern history, English, journalism, mathematics and law. Dieter's homeroom teacher introduces Dieter as the school's special guest and a full member of this year's graduating class. She tells her 30 grade 12 students that this year could be one of the best in their lives. It will also be the last year they will all be together. After school Dieter walks with Bree and Chris down to the bay to meet some friends at the skateboard park. When they arrive, there are a few boys clinging to the edge of a smooth cement crater. They skate down the curving sides of the bowl to the centre, where there is a large round hump and then flip and turn in midair to skate back. Dieter and Bree watch from the sidelines.

"Did you ever get to see it?" Bree asks. They've decided to lie on the grass bank that leads down to the beach. The smell of oil and gas rises on the wind from the marina at the far end of the bay.

"All my life they tell me there is the wall," Dieter says, "and then last year it comes down. I had been only one time to Berlin, as a child."

"But it was big, wasn't it?" Bree asks. "It was a real wall, not just some yellow line painted on the ground?"

"It was a real wall."

"You are so lucky."

Bree and Chris walk past Dieter's house on the way home. Dieter points it out and tells them his room is on the second floor. Chris tells him he's crazy and purses his lips together to inhale deeply, holding the air in his lungs for a long time and crossing his eyes.

Saturday morning, Mac takes the early shift at the boat rental. Three fishermen show up wanting one of the 14-footers. Mac places their deposit in the till and loads them up with life jackets and a tank of gas. He checks for licences. The men carry thermoses and blankets. Their rods are old, the guides rusty.

"We'll be lucky if we catch bottom," one of the men jokes.

"Enough of that," Mac says.

The day is muted: sunlight, the fall air, the engine's watery exhaust. Mac can tell these are not seasoned sportsmen. They might as well be boarding a train or buying tickets to a movie. The three step gingerly into the boat with all their gear and within five minutes they disappear around the point.

The fishermen return by 11:00. They have caught two mudsharks, which are lying belly up in their own blood on the flat bottom of the aluminum boat. No one wants the fish so after they leave Mac slips them over the side of the boat and they sink slowly into the darkness under the pilings. He stops at a bar on the way home, a nautical place with an oak ceiling and a wall of windows overlooking the bay. Mac likes to invent cocktail combinations to confuse the bartenders. Today he orders a Peach and Frog. He tells the waiter it's a Harvey Wallbanger with crème de menthe instead of grenadine. Last week he ordered a Chinchilla: an ounce of cinzano in a pint of Guinness. Tomorrow he and Marilyn will drive the eighty miles to Eugene, where his sister lives, so that Marilyn can visit her children.

⌗

Marilyn comes home around seven o'clock, dripping wet. She went out for fish and chips and the chair she was sitting on collapsed, tipping her over the edge of the wharf. The young cook lifted her out. He laid flat on his stomach, reached under her arms and pulled her up. She lost her change purse and a pair of sunglasses. The cook said they'd send a diver down for them in the morning. People applauded and someone brought a blanket. She thanked the man, but her heart wasn't in it. The water had been so dark and warm, an unexpected blessing, far too brief.

Now she sits across from Dieter's new friend Bree at the kitchen table, the blanket still around her shoulders. She holds a cup of coffee between her hands, circling its brim with her fingers, the handle facing toward them.

"So if all you get is minimum wage," Bree is saying, "how do you live?" Backpacks heavy with schoolbooks lie against the back door like fallen fruit.

"I rent rooms." Marilyn nods her head upward in the direction of Dieter's room.

Bree bends her head down to the table, sips her own coffee without raising the cup. "Dieter says they're your kids' rooms."

"They are," Marilyn says.

"And that man who made dinner tonight, the old guy. I sometimes see him at the marina. Dieter says he works there."

"He does," Marilyn says.

"Is he, like, your father or something?" Bree asks.

"My uncle," Marilyn says.

Dieter returns from the bathroom and sits down. Marilyn knows he and Bree are being solicitous because of her mishap, but she has no wish to talk to either of them. Mac is in the den reading.

"Your house got busted, right?" Bree asks.

"About a year ago," Marilyn says.

Dieter is smiling across at her. He holds a cigarette aloft in one hand as though he is posing for a photo.

"And that's why your children don't live with you anymore, right?" Bree takes the cigarette from Dieter and puts it out.

"They're with my parents until my probation ends. Maybe sooner," Marilyn says.

"Harsh," Bree says.

Nobody believes Marilyn could have lived in the same house with Evan and not known what he was up to. Her own parents have said that she should have gone to jail too. She thought Evan was building an addition. That was what he did for a living: sundecks, garages, basement suites. Why shouldn't he do it at home? There was plumbing, there was wiring, there was wood, there were nails. It was a lot like their marriage. There were children, a house, a 10-year anniversary, every outward sign it was solid and durable. To his credit, Evan did his best to avoid implicating Marilyn. She was given two years of probation. If Child Services hadn't been alerted to her case, Marilyn might have considered herself lucky.

"I should get to bed," Marilyn says. She rises and heads down the hallway to her room.

"Have a bath," Bree says.

The next day, Marilyn is too sick to stand. She debates having

Mac and Dieter carry her to the car so that she can make the two-hour trip to see Karen and Daniel. It is never a good idea to cancel a scheduled visit, but in the end she phones to say she cannot go.

The night of the Rotary dinner, Dieter, Bree, Marilyn and Mac climb into the still immaculate interior of Evan's '72 Cutlass Supreme and drive two miles to the Newport Trav-L-Lodge, recently renovated to offer full convention facilities. The sun is still perched above the Pacific when they arrive. It is the last day of summer, the equinox. Patches of evening fog swirl past, blown inland by the offshore breeze, pale wisps that wrap themselves around poles, the aerials of parked cars. Dieter is giving a speech tonight and everyone has dressed for the occasion. Mac pressed his grey flannels and polished his Rockports. Marilyn traded her jeans for a white wrap-around skirt. Bree is wearing a full-length black dress that stops just above her boots. Her hair has grown slightly from the close shave she treated herself to at the beginning of school. Mac lent Dieter a sports jacket to go with his white shirt and corduroys.

They troop through a small lobby and stop at a table to pick up name tags. The man in charge writes in bold block letters with a black felt pen and peels off the Teflon strip. Bree places hers immediately on her forehead. They walk into the Buccaneer Room. Heavy rope nets hang from the ceiling, hiding duct work and plumbing. The walls have been painted with tropical scenes of palm-covered islands and sailing ships flying skull-and-crossbones. The prow of a wooden lifeboat protrudes halfway into the room. It's the buffet. The pirate theme depresses Marilyn, until she remembers Karen's postcard and then she perks right up. Bree weaves through the room to a table near the podium and the others follow. "We won't miss a word here," she says.

Each table seats eight. Two carafes of wine — one red, one white — stand in the middle of each table. A few people are seated already, their glasses full, but many more are in a line for the bar. Mac crosses the carpet to join it. A couple of men in suits approach Marilyn and Dieter.

"Hey," one man says.

"You made it," says the other. He looks at Dieter's name tag. "Dieter, isn't it?" he asks, rhyming Dieter with "lighter."

"Yes, but . . . ," Dieter says.

"I'm Peter Trippet. This is John Prentice." There is a flurry of handshaking.

"Look," John says. "You've really drawn a crowd tonight. People are coming out of the woodwork for this. Can I get you something, Mrs . . . ?" He looks in vain at her chest.

"Morgan," Marilyn says.

"Can I get you something to drink, Mrs. Morgan?" he asks.

"Sure," Marilyn says. "That'd be nice. How about a Chinchilla?"

"Sounds good," John says. He turns to Bree. "How about you, Miss? Dieter? Coke okay?"

Peter Trippet explains the schedule of events to them: introductions, dinner, the treasurer's report, three short talks by members of the public speaking club and finally their star attraction, Dieter, who will be speaking on the effects of unification. "So, enjoy," he says before working his way to the podium.

John returns a few minutes later with Marilyn's drink and two cokes for Dieter and Bree. "The bartender was stumped," he tells Marilyn, "until this gentleman filled him in."

Mac sits down with a drink of his own.

"What do you have there?" Marilyn asks him.

"A Thumbelina," Mac says.

Table numbers are drawn out of a hat to see who goes to the buffet first. Beside Marilyn sit the president of the local branch of the Bank of America and his wife. Another man who introduces himself as an accountant for Weyerhauser also joins the table. The chair to Bree's right remains empty. The bank president has been told that Marilyn runs the boarding house where the guest speaker is staying and he tells her he is pleased to see the spirit of free enterprise alive and well in Newport.

"Alive, anyway," Marilyn says. She feels his eyes staring at her hand, the sudden weight of her wedding ring.

"What about your husband?" he asks. "What does he do?"

"He's dead," she says.

Their table number is called. They pick up plates and walk past bean salads and cold cuts, crab legs and lasagne, roast potatoes, lamb curry and a chef slicing off slabs of beef. Everyone takes a little of everything, except Bree, whose plate bears only Caesar salad, two potatoes and bread. They return to find that the waiters have replaced empty carafes with full ones.

"It's on railway tracks," Bree is saying to the accountant as she sits down. "Every room moves but the bathroom."

"I see," the accountant says.

When the police burst through both the front and back doors of the house on that muggy July Saturday, Marilyn was at the King Koin laundromat sorting through a basket of work socks, dividing them into keepers, menders and hopeless. She had dropped Karen and Daniel off for the day at a friend's. She'd left Evan up in the attic hammering. Probably he hadn't heard them knocking, if they had knocked at all. Marilyn likes to believe there was a certain amount of civility — she avoids the word *raid* — perhaps a polite tap at the window first, a shout through the screen door off the back deck. She doesn't see any guns or dogs or nightsticks in her version of things and while she is familiar with the pale gear of the Oregon State Police, she prefers to think of the intruders wearing faded jeans and workshirts. When she arrived home from doing the laundry, she found a small crowd of people gathered outside her house. A few neighbours recognized her and waved as she pulled up. Marilyn ran from the car to the house, her only thought that Evan had started a house fire. She expected to see smoke billowing out from under the eaves and she was relieved when she remembered where the children were. The fire scenario — Evan with a plumbing torch, igniting one of the beams or rafters — preoccupied her as she stepped over the front door, wrenched from its hinges. Once inside, she saw furniture turned over, pictures pulled from the walls, plants torn out by the roots and soil emptied from pots onto the carpets. The fire in her mind was becoming a crazy fire, a fire that eluded capture, one that had to be chased through all the rooms of the house. Evan was nowhere to be seen. It wasn't until she went out into the backyard and asked an officer taking notes what had happened that she found out the truth. He gave her a card and a number to call and when she asked him if she was going to be arrested too, he said "Not today."

⌗

The third of the three public speakers is a teenage girl in a wheelchair. She speaks about her life before the accident, the teams she played on. She describes a typical Friday night with her friends and how a single error in judgement changed everything. At the end of her speech, she repeats the word "forever," allowing a pause of several seconds between the words. Dieter begins clapping immediately and so enthusiastically the whole room soon joins in. Some seem to be confused about what they are clapping for, steeped as they are by now in several carafes of wine, but clap anyway. Two men lift the girl, wheelchair and all, from the platform that serves as a stage and Peter Trippet readjusts the microphone. Then it is Dieter's turn.

People are stirring cups of coffee and several conversations have grown in volume to arguments, when Dieter starts to address the crowd. "It is for me a great joy tonight to speak to you about my country," he says over the rising din. "Since I am young," Dieter continues, "my family has told stories about people who once were our friends and neighbours."

"Louder!" someone in the back yells.

Dieter waves at the person and leans closer to the microphone. "These people disappeared when Germany was cut into two."

"Good riddance," a man behind Marilyn heckles.

"Nobody has seen them for 40 years," Dieter says. "This is an awful thing for your friends to be somewhere else."

Marilyn finds she cannot concentrate on Dieter's words. She squints to block out everything except his face. She cups her hands around her ears, but it does no good. Snatches of his speech drift in and out like snowflakes passing through a beam of light. "The wall was everywhere," she hears him say, "not just Berlin. Missiles in the streets of my town."

She glances at Mac sitting next to her. He is taking small sips of coffee. To Mac's right, she sees Bree with her dress hiked up and her legs crossed in a half-lotus. She rests one boot assertively on top of her right knee. Her hands are clasped behind her neck and she is chewing a piece of gum. Tomorrow is autumn, Marilyn remembers. We are passing from one season to another at this very moment. She pictures the equinox like a curtain suspended in space, the Earth moving through it to the other side. She once believed she was able to detect the rotation of the Earth by looking at the sky through her bedroom window, but a friend pointed out that the clouds passing gave her the *impression* of movement. Marilyn closes her eyes, shutting out Dieter, the drunken Rotarians. She leans back heavily, sinking into the armrests, imagines a wind blowing the hair from her face, the fall giving way invisibly before her.

Although the picture in the paper the next day shows Dieter with his face in Marilyn's lap, her hands supporting it, a better angle would have revealed his body lying on the table so that only his head and neck, possibly one of his shoulders, were guilty of any impropriety. An even wider view would have captured Bree with her left leg fully extended and the tip of one steel-toed boot about to make contact with the stomach of the rude and heavily intoxicated war veteran who, in a fit of pique, staggered to the podium and dragged Dieter from his perch, hurling him across the special guest's table, past the accountant, the bank president and his wife, almost into the arms or lap of Marilyn, who had just awoken from a soothing reverie about time and space to see Mac doing his best to pin the rude man's arms behind his back and Peter Trippet yanking at Bree's dress.

"Fascist!" Bree is screaming at the man. "You stupid fuck!"

For his part, the veteran is yelling even more loudly. "Dumb-ass Kraut," he spits at Dieter, who is still trying to extricate himself from tablecloth, glasses, cutlery. "I'll show you missiles," he says. "I'll show you fucking bombs."

The crowd thins. People pick up hats and purses, don jackets, prepare to slip out the double-doored exit at the side of the room. Marilyn looks down at Dieter struggling to right himself. *As young as he is,* she thinks, *there is something old about this boy, the folds of skin that crease the back of his neck, perhaps — something very European, certainly* — and she lifts his head gently, the way she would a bowl of fruit, so that it's right in line with the lens of the camera.

# KRAUT

I was in grade six when I met Randy. It was the last year of "the bucket lady," the same year Mr. Ranallo came to the school, 1964. We had a house by the graveyard then, a place like a sieve. Wind blew in from Ross Bay all winter long, right through the windows of my room at the front of the house. Sometimes at night, when it rained, I'd wake up to pools of water beside my bed. It was so damp there was condensation on the lens of my telescope. Lights went out when I plugged in the toaster. I was afraid of the wood furnace. My father kept saying he couldn't believe he'd paid good money for a house like this.

Randy's a German. The first thing he tells me is his father was a tank commander under Rommel. "He killed a lot of English soldiers," Randy says. "He had to. He blew them up. He burned them alive in their tanks."

"Who cares?" I say. My father won't talk about what he did in the war.

"He has pictures," Randy says. "Maybe I'll show them to you."

Randy carries German books around with him and reads them when the rest of us are playing catch at recess. One of them has Adolf Hitler's name on it. He sits in the shade of the bicycle racks and turns the pages slowly, sometimes flipping back a few to check on something or writing in a pad he keeps with him. I think he's just showing off, faking all the reading and the writing just to get our attention. I watch him to see if he looks our way, but he never does.

Mr. Ranallo is our teacher. He's Italian. He's also young. Since grade one, I've had only war veterans for teachers, old guys who still have shrapnel and Plexiglas stuck in their heads, so at the assembly on the first day of school, Mr. Ranallo is pretty easy to pick out. He's standing on the stage looking like Paul Anka or Bobby Darin. For once we have a teacher who looks like he can kick a soccer ball without having a heart attack. Last year, when the grade sevens were practising after school, they had to call an ambulance for Mr. Boyes. I remember they drove it right onto the field. The soccer team and a couple of janitors were standing over him.

Everyone wants into Mr. Ranallo's class, so I guess you could say I'm lucky because, when they finish calling all the students' names, I'm sitting on a bench right behind him with most of the toughest and stupidest kids in my grade. It must be the luck of the draw, because I'm not stupid. I'm not much of a fighter either. Once, a teacher called me a wise-ass because when I sneezed I made a noise like a donkey. Since then, all the teachers think I'm a class clown and put me in with Stephen Prescott and Gary Butler. It's probably somebody's idea of a lesson. But who cares? I'd rather be in a class with these idiots than with Mary Borsini and Chris Tomkins. They're looking pretty choked right now because they have Mr. Love for the second year in a row. He's the principal. When the assembly's over, he tells us not to forget to come back tomorrow. It's the same joke he used last year.

Bucket lady's digging up her lawn again. She's carrying the dirt down to the beach in her rusty buckets. She's wearing her dirty brown overcoat and her big black hat. Her hair's all tangled and grey like a witch's and she's singing about the queen of England. I watch her from the front window just like I watch my dad on his way to work. People say she has a stepfather back at the house who shouts orders at her from his sickbed. They say he makes her life so miserable she has to take out her problems on the lawn. She hacks at it with her hands, tears it up in clumps and totes it down our street to the bay. She'll make two or three trips in an afternoon. I just watch her. Sometimes I yell at her. I yell whatever comes into my mind. "Hey, bucket lady," I say. "Happy Thanksgiving," I yell.

Every year there's one day she doesn't carry her buckets, but I can never predict it. Then she goes away for a long time. Her lawn grows back with crab grass and weeds. In the spring she comes back again. There she is, on her knees, fertilizing, adding topsoil, pulling out dandelions and buttercups, doing her best to fix the damage.

"Nice grass," I said to her when she came home this time. I thought it was the sort of thing she would want to hear.

"Yes, it is," she said.

"Keeping it this year?" I asked.

"Go away, boy," she said and her hands started weeding like crazy.

Now she's back to her old tricks, singing and ripping out grass and dumping her buckets into the sea.

⌗

The day after registration, I get a better look at Mr. Ranallo. He's what my father likes to call "beefy," a big chest and hair like motor oil. He's wearing a black suit, a white shirt and a tie. We sit down and he starts filling out his register. I take my supplies from the big paper bag they come in at Eaton's — five notebooks, a *Gage Canadian Dictionary*, scissors, paste, a geometry set, a Pink Pearl eraser — and put them in the desk he's assigned to me.

"Fuck me, asswipe," Frank Henson says when I watch him pick the wax out of his ear, but otherwise nobody says anything. There's a knock and the secretary brings in another student. It's Randy. He goes right to the blackboard, picks up a piece of chalk and writes his name in block letters, just his first name. Then he swallows the chalk.

We all expect Mr. Ranallo to kill him. It's only nine o'clock on the first day. No teacher can let a kid get away with something like that; everybody waits for him to take out the strap. A teacher can hit you up to 15 times as long as your hands aren't lying on a table or any hard surface. They'd smash your fingers to pulp if they did that. The sun's coming in through the three big windows and Randy's standing there blinking and smiling, his hands behind his back like he's getting an award. He has a goofy look in his eyes, like he's Danny Kaye or one of those French mimes. He thinks he's pulled it off, nothing mean or cruel, just harmless. Mr. Ranallo looks at the board and then at Randy.

"Say hello to Randy, class," he says.

"Hello, Randy," we all say.

"Do you have a lunch with you today, Randy?" Mr. Ranallo asks.

"Yes, sir," Randy says and then he salutes.

"Good," Mr. Ranallo says. "Now, take a seat."

A month ago, my father got a job longshoring with CP Rail, a good deal for us because he hasn't had much luck with a steady paycheque. He says all the immigrants are taking the work away from *real* Canadians. He won't let us buy a box of Japanese oranges at Christmas because of what the Japanese did to us. And he'd never buy a Volkswagen. Now he's bringing home watermelons and bags of peanuts and whole sacks of corn he says come with the job.

They met before the war, my mom and dad. In high school. They got married in 1939 and then they didn't see each other for seven years. My dad doesn't tell a lot of stories. He never talks about what it was like in the army or what he did when he was my age. But sometimes, when he has a beer and a few friends are over, he'll tell us about the first time he saw my mom coming down the stairs at the school and how he knew he was going to marry her. You can see my mother likes to hear him tell it too. She wags her finger at him and gets out the yearbook to prove him wrong on something. Sometimes she flips to the sports teams and points out the guys she gave up for him, laughing, but sometimes she gets up and goes into the kitchen and busies herself with dishes or baking.

She takes courses at the college when she can, psychology and counselling courses. She says one day she's going to get her degree and a job in social work. A real job, she says, but my father just laughs.

On weekends she pokes around in the garden at the side of our house and my father puts on his coveralls and works underneath his truck. Almost every Sunday we go for a drive, out of town to a beach or a park where there's a hiking trail and usually we stop for lunch somewhere. Last Sunday we went to see the Indians race their war canoes at the reserve. My dad grew up beside a reserve, so he always likes to see what the Indians are up to. We had to get there early to find a place to sit where we could see the harbour. The Indians were selling hot dogs and corn on the cob, a few people had brought coolers of beer. After about an hour, my dad left us sitting on our blanket and started talking to some men down by the water. I saw him give the men some money and then he came back. On the way home, he bought us all ice cream at the Bright Spot.

I like my dad. He comes outside at night when I've got my telescope on the lawn and we talk about the stars. Once he showed me how to find Betelgeuse.

When I get home the first day of school, I find my mom in the backyard standing under the apple tree. She looks angry at the tree, like she's going to yell at it, but she's just catching apples my dad is throwing down to her. He's home early for a change. The apple tree is taller than the house. My mother uses both hands to catch the apples. She puts each one in a box that my dad carries into the basement. He lays them out on newspaper so they'll keep. The apples my dad can't reach he gets with a cloth bag at the end of a stick. The bag is threaded onto a clothes hanger that's been shaped into a circle and then nailed to the stick. He just slips the bag over an apple and pulls. After I get there, my mom says she's tired of catching apples.

"Put the kid on it," my father says.

"Him?" my mother asks. "He can't catch."

"I bet he could if we paid him," my father says.

"What do you say, kid?" my mother asks. "A penny an apple sound fair?"

When she finally calls us in for dinner, I've made over a dollar.

As soon as Mr. Ranallo tells Randy to sit down, we stop listening to him. We stop paying attention when he asks us to work, to take our seats, to be quiet. We stop being scared of him. The whole class starts taking advantage of Mr. Ranallo's good nature, a trait my mother says we should really be thankful for. She says that children can't tell when they're lucky, that we have no idea what luck is, in fact. She says we know who we know and live where we live. She says it's a blessing; otherwise, we might refuse to grow up. One of her psychology courses probably taught her this. On top of all the talking and paper throwing and not sitting in the right desks, Randy follows Mr. Ranallo everywhere. I think Randy is just showing how far he can go, acting like Harpo Marx when he puts his head on Mr. Ranallo's shoulder.

"You must work harder, people," Mr. Ranallo says. "You will be useless," he warns us. "The world will eat you alive."

And then Randy gets out of his desk and tells Mr. Ranallo everything is okay. He leans his head into Mr. Ranallo's neck and strokes his arm or his shoulder.

We sing a lot in Mr. Ranallo's class. Mr. Ranallo holds his guitar high against his chest like Ricky Ricardo on *I Love Lucy*. He moves up and down the aisles between our desks singing folk songs. His voice is deep and rich and strong. He sings about Froggie going courting and Michael in his boat. When he stops singing, we stop working, so Mr. Ranallo sings all morning. In the afternoon, we draw or play soccer.

One day the police come to school to take Randy away for something he did. They don't say what it is, but we all know he's the one who painted the big swastika on the back wall of the new Safeway. Mr. Ranallo says he won't let him go until he's finished his math. The police say they can wait, so Mr. Ranallo invites them in. The two policemen sit at the back of the class and listen while Mr. Ranallo sings "Lemon Tree" to us. We're all watching to see if they're going to join in, but they don't. Then they take Randy away and Randy smiles and winks at us as if he's Steve McQueen going back to solitary. After they've gone, the principal calls Mr. Ranallo outside into the hall. Mr. Ranallo winks at us too. Then Randy comes back in with Mr. Ranallo; they're both smiling.

That's when Randy starts laughing out loud. "Okay, the joke's over," Mr. Ranallo says after a minute, but Randy doesn't stop. It gets so bad Mr. Ranallo takes him down to the kindergarten class to sit with the little kids for a while, but we can still hear him.

The next day the principal catches Randy peeing into one of the drinking fountains. Randy can't escape this time, but the principal refuses to strap him. He orders Mr. Ranallo to do it. Nobody sees it. We only get the story later. All we see is Mr. Ranallo coming in after the strapping. His hair's a mess and his tie is loose. Randy comes in a few minutes later, holding his hands carefully, as if he's carrying a couple of my mother's wine glasses. When he sits down, he cradles them in his lap. Then he looks up and asks Mr. Ranallo to sing.

♯

Randy and I start hanging around together one day at the beach. I see him jumping and swinging a stick and because I already know him a little from school, I go over. "Randy," I say.

There's a towel tied around his neck like a cape and he's cutting the heads off kelp plants washed up on the beach. "I'm Ranallo Man," he says. He's talking to a piece of kelp he's holding.

"Okay," I say.

"You think I'm just a dumb pizza pie?" he asks the kelp. "You think I don't see how you make trouble for these nice people? You're one wrong dead guy, mister!" Then he slices off the kelp bulb with his stick.

It's a good game. We play it for the rest of the afternoon. I set up the kelp heads on logs and they become people who have to be executed — bucket lady, our principal, the Russians.

"Bucket lady must die. We must kill her," Randy says. "Ranallo Man says cut off her head!"

We take turns doing the killing. Sometimes a kelp bulb is full of water and we pretend it's blood.

Pretty soon Randy starts coming over to my house. I show him my telescope. It's a cheap one, but it has three lenses and a sun filter, a two-inch refractor that brings the apartment houses across the bay right into focus. It's easy to spy on them because the curtains on the ocean side are always open. I look at passing freighters, too and couples walking along the beach. I see a lot through that eyepiece, let me tell you. I also look at the planets — Jupiter mostly — and the moon. The local observatory hands out free star charts, ones that rotate through the seasons. I spend a lot of time figuring out the constellations. You'd be surprised how often information like that comes in handy. Everywhere I go I see something about Andromeda or Orion or Cassiopeia. Maybe it's only the name of a car or a television, but I know where it comes from, just the same. The sun is my favourite. People take the sun for granted. They think it's always going to be there, but it's just a regular star like all the others. It's got limited fuel and one day it's going to explode.

Randy and I look into apartment windows. Randy makes up stories about the people inside. Stuff I would never think of. He tells me the people in the apartments are Germans like his dad. He says that they're the ones who ran the concentration camps and that they're hiding out in Canada. The way he says it, I almost believe him. We watch them and take notes about them. If they answer the phone, we make a note. If they get up to go to the bathroom, we make a note. We're going to hand over everything to Randy's dad when we've got enough information. Bucket lady comes by sometimes and we look at her. It's almost Hallowe'en and she's still carrying her buckets. Firecrackers are exploding all over the neighbourhood.

Every day after supper, Randy comes over and we go upstairs to spy. My father comes in one day and takes my telescope away when he finds us pointing it at an apartment bedroom. He slaps the tripod together and carries it out of the room as if he's caught us with a *Playboy* magazine. I tell my dad we were only watching the Germans.

"I don't want that Kraut in my house anymore," he says.

I tell Randy we should probably go to his house from now on, but Randy says he's not allowed to have anyone over, so we go back to the beach. We kill more kelp. We kill Mr. Steele, the vice principal and the Chinese grocer who kicks us out of his store. One day Randy kills his father three or four times and I kill my father too. I show him how to dig a deep hole above the high-tide line and cover it with twigs, a piece of newspaper and dry sand so that it looks like there's no hole at all. We hope to trap somebody, break his or her legs if we can, but it never happens. Usually we get bored waiting, so we blindfold each other and wander around the beach until we fall into it ourselves.

The day before Hallowe'en, Randy shows me how his jaw has a double hinge. He can put a whole orange in his mouth. We go outside and walk around the streets until we see a man riding a bicycle. We stop and tell him we're in trouble. When he comes over, Randy opens his mouth and the man lets out a whistle when he sees the orange getting bigger and bigger, as round and bright as the sun. We pretend that the orange is stuck and that Randy's choking. The man tells us to wait and he bicycles home to call a doctor. While he's gone, we run away.

⌗

Hallowe'en comes on a Saturday. This year I'm a Beatle. I have a grey collarless jacket, a black wig and tight black pants. I'm John, Randy is Ringo. Every allowance for the past three weeks has gone for firecrackers and I carry them with me in a paper treat bag slung over one shoulder. When I pass other kids our age, I throw a firecracker at them. We knock on doors and sing lines we know from Beatles songs instead of yelling "Trick or treat."

"Bucket lady," I yell, "I want to hold your hand," but nobody comes to the door. There's no light anywhere and I hear no sound.

"Hey, witch," Randy yells. We light a few firecrackers and leave.

It's a long night.

Randy and I climb the hedge into the graveyard beside my parents' house. Randy says that we should hunt each other in the dark, that we can pretend it's the war and we're commandos on a raid. We move off in different directions. There is no moon. The place has so many trees it's like a forest. It's difficult to run and the wind off the ocean is cold. I crawl under a bush for a while and wait, hoping I'll hear him, but nobody comes close. I move toward the main entrance, up one of the narrow paved roads. When I cross to another road between two small mausoleums, there's an explosion in my ear and my legs are pulled out from under me. I light a match and look at Randy in an open grave below me. He's up to his knees in mud and dirt.

"I could have killed you," he says. "You were as good as dead."

The police come looking for vandals and we take off. At ten o'clock, my father lights the family fireworks. I watch him nail a pinwheel to the pear tree and light it. It spins for a while, then stops. After that it's a few Roman candles, a volcano and a burning schoolhouse. I wave my sparkler, count my candy and go to bed.

⊞

Randy's house is a two-storey grey stucco. Randy lives in the new subdivision next to the park. He says there's a dishwasher and an intercom.

At school Randy told me he had something to show me, so this is what I think I'm here to see. He takes me in through the back door. "My dad's probably sleeping," he says. He leads me to his bedroom. There's a bed, a dresser, a chair covered in clothes, a mirror on one wall, but not much else. No models or pictures, only the German books he carries around at school and a few dirty dishes.

"Isn't he at work?" I ask.

"Who?" Randy asks. He throws himself onto his bed.

"Your dad," I say. "It's Monday. Isn't he working?"

"My dad doesn't work," Randy says.

"Oh," I say. "Sometimes my dad doesn't work either."

"No," Randy says. "That's not what I mean."

"What *do* you mean?" I ask. I sit down on the edge of the bed.

"I mean he doesn't work," Randy says, laughing. "He's broken."

I don't say anything.

"Want to see?" Randy asks, sitting up.

"See what?"

Randy jumps off his bed and takes me up a set of stairs. He puts a finger to his lips and points to the living room. I walk toward the doorway and look in. The room is large, with wooden floors and a fireplace that goes all the way to the ceiling. The wall across from the fireplace is made of wood, big panels of it, polished and smooth. There's a television in one corner and a wheelchair sitting a few feet away. I can see a head and arms but no legs. When I turn back to Randy, he's looking for something in a drawer by the sink.

"Watch this," he says. He takes a can of lighter fluid from the drawer and unscrews the cap. He squirts fluid along both of his arms. From the drawer he takes a box of matches. He stands by the living room door and looks at me.

"Dad!" he shouts. "Help me! I'm on fire!" Then he takes a match from the box and lights it. He holds the match first to one sleeve and then to the other. "Dad!" he shouts again. "I'm on fire!"

He runs into the room and dances around his father, who suddenly spins his wheelchair. His father doesn't speak, only waves his arms. His mouth is a scream, but there's no noise. Randy dances in circles and weak blue flames rise from his shirt. They look like feathers. His father wheels toward him and Randy backs away. "Help me!" Randy says, but he's laughing too.

I'm not sure what he wants me to do now — watch, laugh at his father, set myself on fire. I find the back door, close it behind me, but I can't make myself go home. I walk around to the front steps and peer in the large picture window just beside the front door, careful to keep my head low.

For a minute I think Randy has left the room, that he's looking for me, but then I see he hasn't left after all. He's still in the living room, crouching on the floor. The fire from the lighter fluid has died out and Randy is kneeling with his head on his father's lap. His father is stroking Randy's hair and shoulders. Randy's face is turned toward the window, the same look on it Randy had when he swallowed the chalk, and he doesn't see me at all.

# THE DAY THE
# LAKE WENT DOWN

I pulled up in front of Willy's house and idled, thinking Willy might be watching for me, but he wasn't, so I leaned on the horn. A blind went up in the house next door, the Dutch deckhand again, spitting at me out the window, waving his useless arm. Government trucks have that effect on some people. I saw him with a pen and paper once, pretending to write down my plate number. He could have written a novel in the time it took him. Nobody at the Ministry of Forests would ever listen to a crippled old drunk anyway. And even if they would, I didn't care. I wasn't going to get out of the truck and knock on the door.

There was another step broken since I'd last been here and more shingles had fallen from the roof. Somebody had dumped a couch on the strip of grass between the front steps and the sidewalk. Its legs were gone.

Willy came out after the second blast, one arm through the sleeve of his red lumberjack shirt, a cigarette in the other hand and a bag lunch hanging between his teeth.

"Hey, college boy," he said. It's what he always says.

I reached across and lifted the lock on the passenger door. "Hey, Willy," I said.

He slid onto the seat. Willy smelled like a can of beer that somebody had pissed in and left in the sun, a few cigarette butts swilling around at the bottom. I figured it was in his skin or his lungs, something that leaked out of him. I rolled down the window.

"Sorry, I didn't see you. I was busy."

"It's okay, Willy."

Willy pulled up the front of his shirt and showed me his stomach. It was covered in blood, smeared in some places and speckled higher up. There was even blood in his beard.

"Willy, what's the matter with you?"

"Nothing," he said. Then there was a wheeze of a laugh and he threw the last of his cigarette out the window. "Things get a bit sloppy when they're on the rag, that's all."

"Don't tell me, Willy."

"Sort of like humping a leaky water bed," he said. "Slappety, slap, slop." Willy was laughing so much he was coughing and his lips and his tongue were working to clear the spit from his mouth. "We probably looked like a couple of stuck pigs."

I moved out into traffic and headed for the coast road. It was bad enough having Willy in the same vehicle. Now I had him in my head too: rolling around belly to belly with some barfly, his pants to his knees, blood flying like rain. I drove for the next half hour and Willy smoked. Then he wanted coffee.

"Let's get some breakfast," he said.

I stopped at a marina out by the reserve. The Indians ran a café and boat rental, a place we'd chosen early on because it was out of the way. We were being paid to hide was how I looked at it. There were a few boats tied up at a wharf and fishermen were coming up to gut their catches. I ordered eggs and toast. Willy had brought a beer, so he drank that. The sun was barely over the trees, but it was warm, so we sat outside on a deck above the water where we could hear the old guys down on the dock talking about their engines and the price of gas, tossing fish heads and tails to the seals.

"Hey," I said and I held up my watch. Willy would've stayed all day if I'd let him.

"Bite me," Willy said, but he got up anyway.

Another 45 minutes and we were out at the dam. It was just after nine. No surprises. Today was no different from any other morning. One look told us what we needed to know and we lay down and went to sleep.

⌗

"So," Donna said when I first told her about the job, "buy me some gas for a change?" We were in her bed at her parents' house.

"Sure," I said.

"What a treat," she said.

Donna wanted to take a holiday. My 20th birthday was coming up. She told me she wanted to rent a cabin on a beach somewhere and cook dinners and go for walks. I said it was okay with me, I had money now. That's what she liked to hear.

"You should move too," she said.

I didn't say anything because there were certain things I didn't like to get into with Donna. I was also thinking about her parents, where they were staying in Seattle, some suite they'd rented for their anniversary, probably lying in bed just like us, a tray of room service and a bottle of wine on the dresser. They had no idea their daughter was screwing some guy they wouldn't even hire to cut their lawn. I was thinking about them and looking at the way the ceiling in Donna's room slanted, how rooms like this were a nightmare for drywallers, all those angles, those crazy corners, the hours of sanding.

"No, *you* should move," I said. "Look at those stuffed animals of yours. You've been staring at them for 20 years."

"Your bathroom's disgusting," she said.

I got up to pee.

"You can't smoke in here," she said.

I knew what she meant, but the way it came out made it sound like a fact, a law of physics. "There's an idea," I said and left.

The toilet lid was covered in green carpet and there was another carpet on the floor just like it wrapped around the base of the toilet in a *U*.

"Put something on," she said when I came back into the room.

"Nobody's here," I said.

"I am," she said.

I pulled a cigarette from the pack in my shirt pocket and sat back. I didn't light it, just let it hang from my lips. The dormer window was open and a breeze was blowing back the lace curtains. It felt good to be naked in this room with its Andrew Wyeth reproductions, its posters of the Eiffel Tower, the Russian dolls all lined up ready to jump inside each other and disappear. One wall was covered with black-and-white photos of stones from a wall in an English cathedral Donna had visited with her parents when she was 15. Sometimes it's hard to believe there are actually people who think this is art.

Donna was small with an upturned nose and Twiggy curls. The thing I liked most about her was her knees. They almost weren't there, as if her legs bent by magic.

Someone named Tom had phoned me about the job. When I met him, he showed me a picture of the Ford truck he'd just bought. You could see he didn't really care what I thought. He had very little hair for a young guy and he smoked too much.

Whenever he talked about women, he called them "ladies," even if they were 17 years old. I met him on a Monday morning by the bus depot and he took me out to the government motor pool, where we requisitioned an International crew cab. After that, we picked up Willy. He was sitting on the curb, head between his knees, and at first I thought he was a drunk. When he started to get in the truck, it looked like we were in for trouble, but Tom introduced us and then Willy lay down on the back seat and went to sleep. Tom rolled his eyes a bit and held his nose.

Willy slept the 50 miles to the lake. The last 18 we had to take a private logging road up into the bush. There was a two-way radio under the seat that Tom kept tuned to a company frequency. Every couple of miles or so, a trucker up the road would broadcast his position.

"Mile 10 and loaded," a voice said.

Then Tom reached for the mike. "Mile seven, empty." It was a game of chicken. The trick was to get as close as we could to the logging truck before getting out of its way. Sometimes we'd get off the road just as the truck was coming around a corner, 20 tons of logs chained behind it and a cloud of dust. You could tell that Tom got a kick out of it.

The lake wasn't really a lake. It was a forest that had been flooded, but the trees were still standing even though they were dead. When we got there, Tom nosed the truck onto a bluff above the water. "Hey, Sleeping Beauty," he said to Willy.

Willy pulled himself upright and shook his head. "Fuck you too," he said.

Tom got out and banged the roof. "Chop, chop," he said.

I found out later Tom had a degree in psychology, which made him more interesting to me for a while because he didn't seem any smarter than other people. The first time we were alone on the job together, Willy told me Tom had a stick up his ass.

The three of us walked around the edge of the lake. We followed an overgrown path through salal and willow and marked the contours of the land with red flags. Tom told us the water level was controlled by Hydro. The company was going to drain the lake, he said. That way we could get down into the stand of dead timber and divide it up into sections for private contractors to bid on. Fallers would cut down the snags and buck them into lengths for the mill.

"Why are we doing this?" I asked.

"It doesn't look good," Tom said. "A lake with trees sticking up in it. But it's old growth and just because they're dead doesn't mean the wood is bad."

The only hitch was that Hydro had never said when it was going to drain it. The reservoir was being used as a backup to the main grid, so Hydro would let the water out only when there was no risk of a power shortage.

Since nobody could do anything while the water was high, Tom told us there was no need for him to come out with us every day.

"What do you expect *us* to do?" I asked.

"Watch the lake," he said.

That was the job. Every day I went into town and picked up Willy so we could drive for an hour and a half to see if a hole in the ground was still full of water. Our work was finished the moment we arrived. After that the time was ours to spend any way we wanted as long as we didn't leave the area. Willy slept in the back seat. I brought books Donna had picked out for me. She said I should try to make something of myself. The forestry department had given us an aluminum boat, so I took it out sometimes and rowed between the dead trees. Most were barkless and the wood was silver. I thought the water under the boat looked blacker than normal. It was easy to get lost because there were so many trees. I never rowed far. Other days I didn't get out of the truck. We could see the lake level from where we parked and for weeks it stayed high. If we wanted, we could drive up to the dam and check the depth marker just to make sure, but there was no point.

"Good night, Willy," I'd say when we arrived at the lake.

"Wank away, college boy," Willy said as he climbed into the back seat.

Maybe I'd see a deer or a black bear. The fool hens were always going crazy, limping away like they had broken wings. I read *The Dharma Bums* and *Tortilla Flat*. After that it was *Crime and Punishment*. When it was time to go, I woke Willy for the ride home.

"Make way for the night shift," he said.

"How long you figure we can get away with this?" I asked him one day. "Doing nothing."

"Don't rock the boat, college boy," he said.

If the day was warm, it was hard to sleep. On those days Willy would tell me stories about the women he met in bars, how many drinks they bought him, what he did to them before leaving the bars, what he did after, how many times. He said he was educating me. "A lesson a day with Willy Wonderfuck," he'd say. "How to put a little lead in your pencil. Write this down, there'll be a test at the end of the term." You spend a whole day with someone, you'd think a bit of conversation would be desirable, but I liked it better when he didn't talk at all.

I believed sex was something you paid for. Maybe no money changed hands, but you paid just the same. I paid Donna by letting her make me look like an idiot, by saying yes when she picked out clothes for me, by posing in front of tombstones while she took photographs. When I told her this, she said she didn't make me look like an idiot at all. She said that's just the way I looked. Anybody who saw those pictures would have to agree. Sometimes I was glad just to get away from her, crawl into my own bed. Donna hated the communal house I shared with Tim and Madeline. A realtor friend of a friend was using it as a tax dodge and rented it to us cheap. We tried to be fair about the rent, the heating bill, the hot water. We put a jar on top of the fridge for grocery money — we were all supposed to chip in. There were rules to make sure nobody got stuck doing the dishes more than twice in a row. Tim arranged our records in one big pile by the stereo. Madeline tacked a Maxfield Parish print on the big wall in the living room, a picture of two boys, one of them naked. They were between some classical columns and you could see mountain and ocean in the background. It was called *Daybreak*. Everything was golden and blue. Cerulean, Donna called it when I told her about it.

When Tim got drunk, he'd start talking about how we were a true cooperative. Sometimes he'd say commune and other times he'd go on and on about the collectives he'd been reading about in his Russian history class. I told him we were living pretty much the way we lived when we were at home — we were playing house. He didn't like to hear that. There was a big living room, a kitchen, one bathroom, a bedroom on the main floor (Madeline's). Tim and I built rooms in the basement out of scrap lumber and wallboard and wired in a couple of plugs.

Donna never came right out and accused me of anything, but every once in a while she mentioned something about Madeline having a good thing.

Even my mother dropped hints. "Madeline's a lucky girl," she'd say, "to have two young men looking after her."

And when Willy found out where I lived, he punched me in the shoulder, a friendly but hard punch.

"I'm not sleeping with her, Willy."

"Then you're stupider than I thought," he said.

＃

That summer seemed to go on forever. Fireweed was blossoming in every clearcut and slash burn in the valley. We could smell the stink before we'd driven a mile into the watershed. Bears were rooting around for berries in the bush on the far side of the lake. Our survey tape hung limp in the branches. "Limp as my dick in a roomful of fags," Willy would say. After a few weeks, I could hear his voice before he even opened his mouth. One night in the kitchen, I was washing and Tim and Madeline were drying, and I told them any job that lets a person fuck the dog for eight hours was a hell of a job.

"Excuse me?" Madeline said.

Working with Willy was taking its toll. He was only about 25, but his back was already a little stooped and the skin on his face was a ground-in grey. Nicotine stains didn't even begin to explain the colour of his fingers. His hands were yellow to the palm. He brought two sandwiches of white bread and baloney every day for lunch and a can of beer. Once I asked him what he would do when the job ended.

"College boy," he said, "I am the mud on the underside of the bottom rung of the ladder. Where I go or don't go doesn't mean squat to me or anybody else."

I think he'd rehearsed this. After a week with Willy, I looked at myself in the mirror and all I saw was a kid who was supposed to be in school.

＃

The day the lake went down was also my birthday. I had no intention of telling Willy. I told myself this was what birthdays were like for most people anyway. You went to work, you ate your lunch. You had a secret and you didn't tell anybody.

We pulled in a little after eight. The land was nothing but mud, most of it dry and hard and starting to crack in the rising heat of the morning. The trees were bigger than I'd imagined they were. I climbed down onto the lake bed. Nobody had seen this land for a long time. It disappeared under water the same year the *Titanic* sank. The river Hydro had dammed to make the lake was nothing now, just a muddy slit in the ground. I expected to see dead fish, but there weren't any. The lake had been so foul with rotting bark that nothing could live in it.

Willy and I drove back once we finished our inspection. I guess I was happy to have something to report, so I drove faster than usual and didn't see the deer until it was too late. We'd just passed a logging truck and the dust was still thick in the air when I saw it standing about 20 feet ahead. It didn't move and I couldn't stop. I hit it with the right fender and spun on my brakes into the opposite shoulder. Willy yelled, "Get out of the way," not making any sense because we'd already *hit* the deer. Then he opened his door and jumped out. A few seconds later, another logging truck clipped the tail end of the International and sent me into the ditch.

⌗

When I was released from the emergency ward, I had a broken nose, two bruised ribs and a handful of stitches in my knee, which I'd cut on a beer bottle I'd fallen onto pulling myself out of the wreck. The driver of the logging truck had given us a ride as far as the time keeper's shack by the booming grounds. From there we'd taken a cab to the hospital, but when Willy saw how long we had to wait, he'd called another cab and left.

The police wanted to see the deer and the truck to verify the events. They also wanted to see Willy. I told them he'd gone. After the doctors were through with me, a policeman and I drove all the way back to the scene of the accident and this time Tom came along to oversee the tow. He also wanted to see the lake. By the time we were done, it was past six.

Donna was waiting at my house. She'd rented a room at an upscale hotel on the waterfront for my birthday and wanted to surprise me. But when she saw my bloody nose, the long gash in my jeans and the way I limped toward her, she told me I'd spoiled everything.

"Hey," I said. "I didn't plan this."

"You owe me 40 bucks," she said and got into her car.

Tim and Madeline took me out instead. They bought rounds of beer and sang "Happy Birthday." We ended up at the Kings just before last call. I spotted Willy shooting a game of pool in one corner. I called him over and when he saw the glass of beer I was waving, he joined us.

"It's my birthday," I said and tried to smile, but the pain from my nose made me wince instead.

"Watch out, college boy," he said. "You're starting to look like me."

# DEAD

Anna's friends tell her she got herself a sweet one, as if all boys look the same, like cantaloupes, until you take a bite.

They are sitting around their usual table at the George and Dragon, a medieval coffeeshop that also serves beer and pizza. Three white coffee mugs, rimmed with three different shades of lipstick, steam lazily around an overflowing ashtray. It's only the third week of classes with few assignments; the days are cheap echoes of summer. Anna listens while Claire and Tessa discuss the boy Anna's been seeing for the past two months. They say anyone shorter would be out of the question; the tattoo is in good taste, they both agree, but what's with the armband?; skinny's better than a weight-room freak, even kind of androgynous, which is very cool, but don't be too rough with him or he might break. Anna's new boyfriend is a doll that they take apart, arm by arm, leg by leg.

"Shelf life," Claire says. "That's what you're looking for." A curl of smoke twists in the air above her head like a screen saver.

"Right," Tessa says. "Best before."

"I know," Anna says. "Best before breakfast."

"Lunch," Claire says.

"And dinner," Tessa says, stubbing out her cigarette.

Anna tells them his father cremates people. "He's the guy who burns the bodies," she says. "He grinds them up too." Her friends look at her as though she's just announced an interest in Christ or Mick Jagger.

Claire drains her coffee and reaches for her books. "Time, ladies, please," she says and the three of them leave for class.

It's their last year of high school and no one is happy about it. There's no *time* for anything. A day hardly goes by that her English teacher doesn't make one of his smug remarks about the real world, rent, tuition, career choices. *The party's over, kids.* The grad committee has already circulated a questionnaire about themes for the dance — the last class of the century, perhaps a nod to the past? Should cap and gown replace the grad dress and tux? Anna thinks she might volunteer to help with the yearbook. She finds herself writing her parting words again and again: *Anna Wayman will be the first drunken fuck on the moon. The Posse lives forever. Less than everything is not enough.*

She waits for weekends when Carl, the boy she met on vacation, hitchhikes the 100 miles from his father's house up island to his mother's condominium in James Bay. Every Friday night for the past three weeks, they look for a friend who can spare a bed for an hour, even a gas station with a lockable washroom. It's that or sit outside Starbuck's and smoke.

Yesterday Anna saw him off at a bus stop in town, his day pack disappearing up Douglas Street in the number 50's back window. The night before they went to a party in a condemned house near the university where a few street kids had been squatting before the police kicked them out. Anna had seen a poster, stapled to a telephone pole, inviting everyone to a final trashing. She and Carl arrived early. A couple of thin homeless boys were trying feebly to tear a door from its hinges. One boy clung to the handle and pulled, while the other kicked at the heavy fir panels. The floors were oak, the walls lath and plaster. Anna looked into the bathroom on her way to the backyard and saw a toilet bowl still upright, the water a thin red, feces floating. Carl tore out the railing from the back porch and pushed a broken hot-water tank through one of the basement windows. When the kids from Oak Bay arrived in their Tommy Hilfiger jackets, Carl and Anna decided to leave. Squad cars came to the house three times after they left and there wasn't a wall left standing by daybreak.

At dinner Monday night, Anna's parents discuss hurricanes goose-stepping through the tropics killing thousands, global economic meltdown. A church next to the high school has dusted off its billboard, which invites passing motorists to leave the rat race and ride the highway to God's kingdom. *The mother of all traffic jams is just ahead*, it says.

The next day Anna sleeps through geography. She types out a recipe in data processing and writes a poem in biology:

*Rows of chickweed, an empty apple tree,*
*The long fingers of our backyard fence.*
*A stalk of fennel, withered, black,*
*The neighbour's cat where raspberries*
*Used to hang.*

After the last bell, she walks home alone, makes a pot of tea and sits on her bed with the door closed. In a while her mother will come up the front steps into the foyer and later her father will arrive home. She has no idea where her brother is. She opens a photo album and flips through the pages: her trip to France in grade ten. She sees herself sipping a strawberry beer in the

Dordogne; the cheese factory in Aurillac, its slabs of *cantal* stacked like checkers, the people there holding their noses; the one of her giving the Eiffel Tower the finger. She flips ahead a few pages: a more recent Anna this time, on a long white beach. She has her arm around Carl, the mountains of the mainland in the background. They've built a castle complete with moat and an evergreen flag. Her father's shadow crawls toward them on the sand. Anna closes the book and pours another cup of tea. She slides down into the covers.

⌗

When Anna's parents rented a cabin outside Parksville for two weeks in late July, they gave Anna the option of staying with friends in town or going with them. But really there was no option. Her father said it might be the last chance for all of them to be together. Next summer she'd surely have a job and after that, well, who knew? They loaded up the roof rack, bolted a couple of bicycles to the rear and hit the road. They stopped to watch some flea-bitten goats eat grass on the roof of a tourist trap that sold Korean wicker chairs and paper lanterns. They bought ice cream at Mom's Diner. They leapt all at once into a riverside pool where they once picnicked when Anna was five.

The cabin they rented was a three-room 40s bungalow with a porch, just one of a collection of shacks that sat like mushrooms, smothered by shade on even the brightest day by a grove of cedars for which the resort was named. Anna carried her suitcase across a sea of needles, a thick, spongy layer of tree crap that rained down hour after hour onto the roof, the thin grass and the car.

The first evening, the oil stove drove them outside: "All that heat just to boil one pot of spaghetti," her mother said. They ate under the cedars, picked out things that fell into their food. Two bottles of red wine convinced Anna's father to tell them again how he once ran into Eric Clapton in a bar in London. *We didn't even talk music, for Christ's sake.* Later the mosquitoes drove them back into the house.

Her parents slept late and after breakfast they read and went wading in the surf. Anna knew the routine; they'd eventually ignore her, leave her to herself. Their intentions were good, but they had no follow-through. Anna's brother made friends in less than an hour and spent the day water-skiing.

Anna walked along the beach to a rock cliff, then turned around and walked the other way until she came to a public park. She headed into town, passed stores, a gas station, a few fruit stands. She bought a magazine and a pop and sat on a bench in the shade, watching people. Bored, she followed the road back to her cabin.

The next day she did the same, except this time, at the cliff, she stopped to look at a boy clinging to the rock face just above the ground. A small bag of chalk hung from his waist and his fingers were white. Anna sat on a log and watched him as he searched the cliffside for handholds, stretched a leg far back behind him into the air and then extended it like a spider's leg to secure a new foothold. Suddenly he let go and fell three feet onto the sand below. He lay there, unmoving.

Anna got up. "Hey," she said. "Hey, there." She walked toward him. "Are you all right?"

The boy lifted himself on his elbows and looked over at Anna. "No," he said. "I'm dead."

"Sweet," Anna said. She came up beside him and dropped to her knees.

"It would have been," he said.

An offshore wind carried the scent of fireweed from hills behind the motel. It was a thick, cloying smell, slightly disgusting, Anna thought, like fast food when you're not hungry. The boy's name was Carl. He lived with his father in a farmhouse, one of the original homesteads. Did she want to see it? He could take her there sometime. There was a quarry too, an acre of holes. Deep ones. She could see those too if she wanted. He was easy, he said. Hey, he was dead. He smeared some chalk onto his face. "Boo," he said. He smeared chalk on Anna's face, the hollows of her cheeks, the wells of her eyes. "Now you're dead too."

He said it in a way Anna had never heard before. She liked its sound, soft, like a pillow hitting another pillow. Everything became distant: the swimmers out in the bay, the families digging for clams. Anna invited Carl for dinner. He accepted. By the end of the vacation, he was eating with Anna's family every night.

On Tuesday Anna tells her mother she's staying at Claire's for the weekend. They have a project due for history. She'll be home for dinner on Sunday. Anna believes in preparing her mother to increase her plan's chance of success. She buys a ticket at the bus depot and packs a bag that she keeps in her locker for the rest of the week. She'll leave after break on Friday. She doesn't feel guilty. It's been a long time since her parents made a real scene. Anna knows that her parents are like the parents of most of her friends: they think of themselves as casual people, tolerant and easygoing. The fact is she rarely has to lie to her parents and she does so only when there's a risk they'll say no. By Wednesday night the odds are in Anna's favour.

On Friday, Carl meets her at the bus stop on the highway. The driver finds her suitcase among all the other baggage in the cargo hold and tosses it to Carl, who staggers a little and says thank you. He has his father's station wagon, a black Mercury from the 60s and he drives her the five miles back to his house. It sits in the middle of a large unkempt field of grass looking out to the sea, a dirty white clapboard building with green trim, a sagging wrap-around verandah and a stone chimney. Anna has seen the house once before. Last summer, Carl's father picked them up walking back along the road to her cabin. He brought them back to the house for a swim.

Carl asks her if she's hungry; his father made some soup and there's a bit of bread too.

"Where is your dad?" Anna asks.

"At work," Carl says.

"Oh," Anna says.

It's Anna's job to put the condom on Carl. Now she uses her mother's word for them. "Let's have another rubber for Mr. Flubber." She makes a joke of it, not because she's embarrassed, but because it's better than waiting for him to remember they need one. Whenever Carl does it, there's a lot of yanking away and plastic wrappers and playing with himself. Half the time he comes before he's even got the thing on.

Anna can't believe there is such a thing as a penis. It's a joke. Would your ear or nose suddenly puff up like a balloon if you liked someone? She tries to imagine some part of her own body bobbing up and down against her will and then she remembers why they're using condoms in the first place. Anna has to be careful not to talk this way to Carl. He hates it when she analyzes everything. For instance, comparisons between what she and Carl do to the mating habits of monkeys or orangutans. It takes the romance out of it, he says, though there's very little romance *in* it as far as Anna can tell. He bounces around for a while on top of her, or behind her, or underneath, and when his eyes glaze over like he's about to pass out, they're finished. *Le petit mort*, her English teacher called it once, "the little death." All Anna knows is she usually has to stop herself from yawning.

When Carl's father comes home, Anna and Carl are lying in front of the television. There's a fire burning in the fireplace and Carl has made a bowl of popcorn. Anna's not sure how long they've been waiting like this, the perfect teenage couple, sharing a snack, watching reruns of *I Love Lucy*, but when the door opens she has to suppress a giggle.

Carl's father is six and a half feet, a gaunt man with a slight bounce in his step, the kind of loping, long-legged stride a person might fall into if the Earth were a trampoline. His hair is long, a little grey, but full. He keeps it tied back in a pony tail. He barely turns his head to acknowledge them lying on the floor. "You again," he says to Anna as he walks through to the kitchen.

"Hey, Ace," Anna says. "Who'd you torch today?"

"Couple of kids," he says, his head in the fridge.

"Oh, yeah?" Anna says.

"Yeah," he says. "They fucked themselves blind and then they walked into a truck." He walks back into the living room with a beer and a plate of cold potatoes.

"Cool," Anna says.

Carl's father lowers himself into a boxy brown armchair that sits across from the TV, the worn-out cushion giving way under his weight. He sets his beer on one arm of the chair and his plate on the other. A music video blares while the last of the twilight fades to black in the picture window overlooking the strait. After Carl's father has finished eating, Anna switches off the TV and gets out the crib board for a three-handed game. They lie on the carpet, their bodies radiating out from the cards in their hands, the board and the nearly empty bowl of popcorn. Carl's father asks why they decided to spend the weekend here.

"It's only fair," says Anna. "Carl's always coming down."

"I don't mind," Carl says. "I really don't."

"Still," Anna says, "you do."

"Fair," Carl's father says, as though the word is foreign.

"Yeah," Anna says. "Besides, the city's dead."

"There's a frightening thought," Carl's father says. "Think of the overtime."

Anna tries to imagine everyone she knows stacked like cordwood in front of a big oven door and Carl's father shoving them one by one into the flames, sweat running down his face, his pockets full of $20 bills. All those people, all the things they do. Up in smoke. Her parents, the fragments of radio programs they bring up for discussion, her father's bottles of homemade Chablis, her mother's dust mop patrolling acres of polished wood floors, cabinets, buffets.

Anna rolls onto her back and draws her knees up to her chest. "The city's dead," she blurts out again between gasps, tears forming in the corners of her eyes. "Christ," she says. "Oh, Jesus."

Carl throws the deck of cards into the air. Diamonds, hearts, clubs and spades flutter to the floor.

Carl's father lurches to his feet and tells them that, if they're not going to share their weed with him, he's going to bed. "Hell," he says. "I'm going anyway."

Later, when the marijuana fades, sleep eludes Anna. Carl is deep in dream beside her. Dead to the world. He shifts positions, drapes one leg over hers. She wonders if she will get to like him one day, perhaps even need him. She tries to imagine him as a man, his face lined, glasses maybe, but all she can see is Carl's father. Would that be so bad?

When Anna first met Carl's father, the day he picked them

up for a swim, a storm was building and she and Carl were walking along the road back to her cabin. The big Mercury pulled up beside them and the driver's window rolled down. "No time to waste," Carl's father said.

Carl had already told Anna what his father did for a living. She was prepared for a suit, a sombre man of the cloth perhaps, not someone in blue jeans and a leather jacket. They arrived at the house when the sky was darkest and thunder sounded directly overhead. Carl's father led them down a path to a rocky beach, where the high waves were breaking on the smooth glacial stone. "Best swim you'll ever have," he said.

Anna watched as Carl's father stripped first to his underwear and then to nothing at all. He was older than her own father, taller too. The hair on his shoulders and back made her uncomfortable. He plunged into the breakers and surfaced about 10 yards from shore. The water was a luminescent green beneath the lightning, rain and pendulous black clouds.

"Come on in," he shouted.

"Don't people get killed doing this?" Anna yelled back at him.

"All the time," he said.

Only after Carl persuaded Anna that the water was warm did she relax and dive in and even then still wearing her shorts and T-shirt.

"It's like silk," she said as the sky flashed and the sweet rain fell right into her mouth.

Carl's father had skin that lay in small folds around his waist. His calves and thighs seemed translucent.

Now she feels Carl's leg on hers, the spare, hard muscle she first saw straining to maintain its grip on a wall of rock. Will she ever have to watch it soften, sag, let go of the bone?

⌗

On Saturday morning Anna tells Carl she has to do her homework, so they spend a few hours around the kitchen table while Anna finishes math and English. She is supposed to be reading *Catcher in the Rye*, but everyone in the book seems so obvious, stupid. If Anna wrote, she'd never write about people. Writers think people are fascinating, but they're really not.

In the afternoon Carl drives Anna out to the rock quarry to see dozens of perfectly round holes in the ground. Carl tells her each hole is exactly six feet wide. They vary in depth, but it's hard to tell because they're full of rainwater.

"In a thousand years," Carl says, "people won't know why these are here. They'll probably think we used them for baths."

"We should," Anna says.

"Or cooking," Carl says. "Big outdoor pots."

"Or graves," Anna says. "They'll think they were graves."

On the way back to the house, Carl pulls into Arbutus Memorial Park, where his father works. He tells Anna his dad will show them around if it's not too busy. The pamphlet Anna picks up on their way through the main entrance says the building is art deco with a hint of gothic revival. It lists a chapel, a community mausoleum, both an indoor and an outdoor columbarium, as well as a garden of remembrance. The foyer could be the entrance to a hospital, Anna thinks, even a hotel. It's that elegant. "What's a columbarium?" she asks.

Anna learns that, because some people like to witness the act of cremation, the crematorium at Arbutus Memorial is more than just a utilitarian workroom. It has several large windows that look out onto a forest and there are receptacles for flowers. The machinery is stainless steel and brass, the floor a Mexican quarry tile. When Anna enters, she sees Carl's father sitting at a bench before a long metal tray, a pair of tongs in one hand. He is pulling out pieces of metal from a pile of ash and bone.

"I've got to put this guy through the grinder by this evening," he tells them. "Any metal bits like the coffin handles have to be removed. They gum up the works."

"Why burn the coffin?" Anna asks. "What's the point?"

"People pay for it," Carl's father says. "And even if we didn't burn it, I'd still have to go through this stuff. A lot of these old guys have steel hips and knees, sometimes plates in their skulls."

Carl has his head in a coffin that sits on a cloth-draped trolley in front of the gas oven. He drops the lid shut, a muted gush of satin air and formaldehyde. He's holding a piece of paper. "It's a picture," he says. "Some kid drew it." He holds it up for them to see. A blue boat, smoke billowing from its stack, rolls across a green ocean.

"Don't go rooting around, Carl," his father says. "The family's coming at four."

"Are you allowed to add stuff like that?" Anna asks.

"People put all kinds of things in there," Carl's father says. " I found a *Playboy* magazine once and a carton of cigarettes."

"He signed it too," Carl says. "For Grandpa, Love Jeremy."

Anna takes the picture from Carl. With a finger she traces the lines of the waves, their simple looping curves. She follows the perimeter of the hull, the smokestack, its rakish, determined angle, the busy plume. A sun in the corner of the paper shines down in long straight rays, yellow as August corn, and a single bird hovers over the bow of the boat. "Who's got a pen?" she asks.

Carl's father pulls one from a coffee cup full of pencils and ballpoints and gives it to her. Anna writes her name under Jeremy's and passes the drawing to Carl, who writes his. Carl's father adds his own before he returns the paper to its place in the coffin.

"A shame to burn it," Carl says. "After all that work."

Anna walks to the window and looks out at the trees. A path winds among a series of low cement structures and beyond them lies a garden. "Which one of these things is a columbarium?" she asks.

Carl's father walks over and points to a free-standing rock wall with row after row of small slots carved into its face. "After they're cremated, we bury the urns in there. It means pigeon holes."

"A birdhouse," Anna says. "A fucking birdhouse for the dead."

It's almost noon before Anna steps onto the bus the next day. She kisses Carl goodbye at the foot of the stairs, a simple kiss, quick, as though they've been married for years. From her seat by the window, as the bus is pulling away, she sees Carl at the side of the road, his hand raised in a wave. He could be anyone. Some of the passengers are watching her. She feels their eyes turned toward her, the force of their expectation. They are waiting for her to wave back. They have reached certain conclusions about what they're seeing and their hope settles on Anna like a shroud.

# THE NEW WORLD

I could live with myself if I didn't help, Rachel thought, but what kind of person would I be? The car passed under a blackened trestle and into another corridor of warehouses, their steam vents busy, a row of anxious plumes on the rise. Everything told her to keep driving, but without signalling she pulled into a vacant bus stop and flipped on the hazards.

Her 28-year-old daughter turned in the passenger seat. "What are you doing?" Avril asked.

"I'll just be a minute. Wait here if you want."

Rachel unbuckled herself and opened the door, her purse on the seat behind her. She paused and looked back up the hill: no bus coming. It was, clearly, the right thing to do. She stepped out of the blue Dodge Colt onto the gritty, rutted street that passed through the city's largest industrial park. Avril stayed put, busied herself with the magazines in her briefcase, rearranging them by volume and issue numbers. It was the kind of self-absorbed activity Rachel knew she was meant to interpret as indifference or mild impatience. Rachel buttoned her coat tightly against the wind and for a few seconds she watched through the glass as Avril's fingers shuffled the stack of magazines again and again, each time more forcefully.

Rachel had spied the cat out of the corner of her eye, a familiar casualty on these long stretches of highway. Usually, she saw the tell-tale grey or brown fur in time to avert her eyes and avoid the sight of mangled flesh. This time, however, she'd been too busy arguing with Avril. The cat was dragging itself across the boulevard. It stood once and then fell. She saw all of this in a millisecond as they passed it. Then she stopped.

Rachel went to the trunk and took out an old blanket she kept there for emergencies. It was the same blanket that lurked in many photographs of family picnics at Ardmore Beach, the same one in the shot of all of them on a hayride the year before she had to sell the farm. Avril had wrapped herself up like a mummy, with only her head showing.

Rachel started walking the 100 yards toward the cat. She was glad to be out of the car, moving her legs, the weight of her feet on the ground a relief. The cold north wind had desiccated the landscape and capricious whirlwinds of dust scuttled between buildings and across the asphalt in front of her. It bothered Rachel that Avril was angry. She hadn't meant to upset her. More and more, though, she found it hard to believe that Avril was her child, that the two of them had once spent whole days in a single room, weeks at a time on the farm alone.

"Don't you want to see Dad again?" Avril had asked earlier. They were returning from a tea with some of Avril's friends.

"That's like asking do I want to live forever," Rachel had said. "Or do I want peace on Earth."

"Well, don't you?"

"I'd like to fly too, Avril, but wanting something isn't going to make it happen."

For a while there was silence and then Avril started in. "That's all you can say, isn't it?"

"Avril, don't."

"Isn't that what you've always said to me? Don't? 'Don't get your hopes up, Avril. Don't ask for too much and you'll never be disappointed.' I never realized how selfish you are. If you can't be happy, then nobody around you can be either. Especially me."

"That's not true," Rachel said, but her words sounded weak.

"I didn't ask you out today because I wanted to. If it was up to me, I'd leave you for God to deal with. He's the only one with enough patience."

"Thanks," Rachel said.

"But I didn't," Avril said. "I made myself phone you because everybody deserves a chance. Those people were so nice and all you could do was make fun of them."

"I didn't make fun of them," Rachel said.

"You treated them like children. Like they still believe in fairy tales."

Rachel said, "All religion *is* a fairy tale."

"So what does that make me?" Avril asked, her hands spread out flat across her knees.

*Stupider than I thought*, Rachel said to herself.

"Sometimes," Avril continued, "I don't understand why you don't just kill yourself."

"Might surprise you yet," said Rachel.

Avril started to cry. She apologized for saying such a horrible thing. She said if Rachel would only come to another meeting with her, she had books for her to read, tapes to listen to. There were people who could answer her questions. If only she'd give it a chance.

*Give it a chance!* Rachel had thought. *If anyone should be angry, it should be me. I was the one who came for tea and got a two-hour Bible lesson.*

⌗

The cat was taking shallow, quick breaths. Rachel walked up to it, not from behind, but facing it, so the cat could see her eyes. In her first glimpse of the creature through the windshield, she'd been certain it must have been hit by a car, but up close now she noticed its fur looked burned and there were nicks on its backside. It smelled of urine. She lay the blanket on the ground in front of the cat. It moaned and closed its eyes. Either it did not have the energy to run away or it trusted her.

On the farm Rachel had helped animals through one sickness or another: sheep were always eating things they shouldn't; Jack, their old horse, had nearly died from a twisted intestine — she'd sat up all night with him, wet his lips with water, contemplated reaching up his ass and unknotting the thing herself if worse came to worst. They couldn't afford a vet. Ultimately they couldn't afford the farm.

She talked to the cat the way she'd talked to Jack, promising relief. If she left it, some highway crew might pick it up and drop it into a plastic bag along with Coke bottles and chip bags. There was little chance Avril would want to help her, not now. *How can she just sit there?* Rachel thought. *Is there a gene for stubbornness?* She looked to where the car was parked and saw Avril's head, a silhouette framed in the back window of the Colt. She was a stranger, an amnesiac, someone who had simply forgotten whole chunks of time. It seemed to be the only explanation. Avril must have forgotten the day she and Rachel combed the forest together for licorice root, the fun they had plucking the small pale-green ferns from the moss that lay thick and damp in the forks of maple trees, later boiling them up on the gas range to make a deep-yellow dye for Avril's dolls' clothes. She must have forgotten how afterward they fed the pulpy cooked roots to the dolls, telling each other it was fairy food that would bring them to life. Forgotten how, on countless afternoons of unremitting coastal rain, the porcelain and rag mouths poured forth secrets of another world until Avril, overwhelmed by her mother's inventiveness, leaned across and put her hand over her mother's lips, a signal she could take no more.

Rachel slipped her hands under the cat and shifted its five or six pounds of bone and sinew onto the blanket. The animal hardly moved. She carried the bundle back to the car, both edges of the blanket clutched together so that it became a sort of sling. She knocked with her elbow on Avril's passenger window. "Open the rear door for me, can you?" She moved away from the car to let Avril out.

Avril looked at her mother's find and then lifted the lock to pull open the door. "It's dying?" she asked.

"Probably," Rachel said. "Yes, I think it might be." Her words were considered, their only intent to be precise, but Rachel heard their coldness too. She heard the careful distance that had imposed itself between her tongue and her heart, the habit of the farm still strong in her, the habit of Harris, her dead husband. "I'd like to keep him lying down on the seat. Could you sit back here and make sure the blanket covers him in case he tries to bolt? It should be enough to hold him, in his condition. I'll do it if you'd rather drive."

"No. Yes. I mean I don't mind." Avril squeezed in beside the cat. "What will you do now?"

Rachel walked around to the driver's side and buckled herself in. She started the car. "I'll take you home first," she said. "You have things to do, I know. Then I'll drop by the SPCA. It's not far and I have another stop near there anyway." She knew Avril was holding herself stiff, tight against the passenger door. The smell of the cat, aggressive, almost menacing, filled the car after only a minute's travel, so Rachel rolled down her window, asked Avril to do the same.

"Do you think you can manage on your own?" Avril asked.

Her daughter's tone was conciliatory, an attempt to appease Rachel after their falling out. Rachel knew that. But Avril's question seemed strangely general, as though now, here in this car and after all these years, her mother's capabilities had suddenly become an issue. And even though she knew Avril was talking about the cat, Rachel felt the question travel deep inside her, like the voice of her husband at the far end of the telephone line, concerned about her. She could feel her shoulders wanting to collapse, fall in on themselves, the fatigue of carrying herself upright too much to bear any longer. She blinked hard and rearranged her hands on the steering wheel. "I'll be fine," Rachel said. "There'll be someone there to help with things."

"I didn't see it," Avril said. "I didn't even hear us hit it."

"We didn't," Rachel said. "Somebody else must have." Stupid, she knew, to mention it, to give Avril another reason to find fault with her — foolish old woman (*not so old,* she told herself) stopping in the middle of nowhere for a stray cat she hadn't even hit.

But Avril said nothing and the rest of the drive was quiet. The cat made a few noises and occasionally tried to lift its head off the blanket. Rachel imagined Avril was still angry with her — *When isn't she?* Rachel thought — but the presence of this animal, its undeniable pain, made argument impossible. *Maybe Avril feels cheated by the cat,* Rachel speculated, *thinks I planned the whole thing to shut her up,* but that was being unfair. She dropped Avril off in front of her house, an older two-storey stucco with a sundeck over the driveway. Avril's son Jerry was shooting baskets, but he stopped and ran over when he saw the car pull up. He would soon be turning eight.

Rachel hunched down, caught Jerry's eye through the passenger window and waved. "Hi, Jerry," she said as he neared the car.

"Hi, Gummy," he said. "Hi, Mom."

Avril eased herself out of the back seat and opened the front passenger door. She leaned across to kiss her mother. She grabbed her purse and the small briefcase and turned around, her free hand quick to brush from her long white coat a strand of cat hair she'd picked up from the blanket. "Jerry," she asked, suddenly aware of her son, "how long have you been home?"

"An hour. We got out early today." He bounced the ball between his legs while he talked.

"I completely forgot," Avril said. "I'm so sorry, sweetheart. Gummy and I were out visiting and I thought we had lots of time. Couldn't you go to Jonah's? Or David's?"

"I didn't want to. You should give me a key."

Avril grabbed the ball away from him and kneeled down to look him in the face. "No, I shouldn't. You should never be home by yourself. Never."

He looked past her, through the rear passenger window. "Is that a cat, Gummy?"

Rachel nodded. "I found it beside the road, Jerry. It's very sick."

Avril stood up. "Gummy's going to take it to the SPCA right after she leaves us. They'll know what to do with it."

"Will it die?" Jerry asked.

Avril looked at her mother.

"Not if it doesn't want to, Jerry," Rachel said. "Animals seem to know when to give up and when not to."

"There's no heaven for animals," Jerry said. "That's what Mom says."

Avril turned away from the car toward the house. "Gummy's not interested, Jerry. She has to go to the vet's and we have to go inside and get you something to eat." She turned briefly back to the car. "I'll call you next week, Mother."

"Goodbye, you two," Rachel said. "Say hello to John for me, will you?" She slipped the car into drive and removed the hand brake. She still marvelled at how effortless driving had become since the '57 International she and Harris had started out with. Its brutish low gear had made the truck's frame jump and shimmy — Harris said it would climb the side of a barn if he let it. He had painted the body himself, with a brush and a can of house paint. Fire-engine red.

Rachel didn't go to the SPCA. She didn't go anywhere near it. As she drove straight home, she realized if Harris were sitting beside her he'd guess in a minute what she was up to. He'd say she was planning to tend the animal herself, that's what he'd say. And he'd be right. He'd call her a fool too. Harris had been making noises in Rachel's head for years. It seemed like she couldn't even sit on the toilet without him trying to get in his two bits' worth. While Harris was alive, the man hardly spoke a word. Now here she was yapping away at the top of her lungs just to keep him from getting a word in edgewise.

Most of this Rachel directed at the cat, reassuring it as well as herself. She talked about other cats she'd had, ones that had fought raccoons or mink and had lived to tell the tale. Somewhere along the way, she decided to tell the cat about Harris's natural distrust of institutions such as banks and hospitals. She related the account of Avril's visit to the animal clinic when she was five. She told the cat how a rabbit had appeared on the front porch one morning and how Avril had actually caught it. The thing was spastic in the hind legs and could only flop about. Harris was all for killing it with a spade, but Avril fought him on it, so finally he agreed to take her to town to talk to the vet. "Talk is all," he said. "No money." The man at the clinic examined the rabbit and pulled back the fur at the base of its neck to show her where a bird, a turkey vulture maybe, had pierced the spine with its claws. Avril told the man that she didn't mind looking after it, that she lived on a farm where it would have lots of company, but he refused to return the rabbit to her care. He told her that he was a member of the SPCA, the Society for the *Prevention* of Cruelty to Animals, and that to give her back the rabbit would only prolong its pain. He wrung the rabbit's neck right in front of her.

Rachel was still talking a blue streak when she pulled down the garage door and turned on the overhead fluorescent light. Her words echoed against the tin of the door. She left the cat lying on the blanket and unlocked the house. She walked all the way through to the living room, where she turned up the thermostat and flipped a few switches, trading one dull light for another. Home is what she was forced to call it when she was leaving someone. "I am going home." She looked around. The TV stood on its stand by the door to the vestibule. A green fold-out couch for guests took up the space beneath the window. There were chairs, pictures, a coffee table, a few things from the farm, a pair of snowshoes, the seven-day clock over the mantel. It might be a still life, she thought, but it's not a home. The clock struck five and Rachel remembered the cat.

Adjoining the garage was a small pantry where she kept a washer and dryer and what the salesman had called an apartment-sized freezer. It was a warm room, with a heat vent right above the furnace. She tore one side off a cardboard box, padded the bottom with an old cushion and placed it next to the vent, just to the left of the freezer. The cat did not object to being moved again and for a moment she thought it must be dead. Its mouth hung open, the tongue lolling. She wouldn't do more than squeeze a bit of clear vitamin E ointment on the cuts and burns. The creature wouldn't do itself any harm that way if it decided to clean itself. She plugged in a night light and set down a bowl half full of water; then she left the cat to fix supper.

An hour later Rachel had stripped the labels from the cans she'd used, washed the cans, set them gleaming, topless and bottomless, in the drain rack along with her plate, knife and fork. In the next hour she would read a little — check in on the cat — and move herself slowly toward the drudgery of bed and sleep. These days all she saw in the dresser mirror before shutting off the bedside lamp was a woman who dithered about dyeing her hair, someone who stared back with the eyes of a cornered rat, buttoned to the neck in a short-sleeved cotton nightgown, trying to fool herself into dreamland.

Once in bed, Rachel took from her purse the small book Avril's friends had pressed into her hands at the end of her visit — *The Truth that Leads to Eternal Life* — and thumbed through it randomly, chuckled at the illustrations of healthy, happy men, women and children, whole families who roamed a pristine countryside with lions and antelope at their sides, the sun above them in a cloudless sky. Such mindless optimism. She had said as much earlier.

"You people aren't farmers," she'd said.

The man, younger than her but balding, a few wisps of hair drawn across his shiny scalp, considered her words and then looked up. "What do you mean?" he'd asked.

"Things die," she said. "Things are always dying. You see that on a farm."

Avril jumped in before he could answer. "That's what we're saying. It's so easy to believe the way things are is the way they have to be."

"I didn't say it was easy," Rachel said. "I said it's what you learn to accept. If you're smart, you do."

Then the man's wife got in on the act. She quoted from

Revelation, said God would wipe every tear from every eye, said there would be no more sorrow and no more pain. The afternoon had gone downhill from there.

Rachel turned to the chapter on the resurrection and stopped at a picture of the dead emerging from the ground, their mouths still fresh with sorrow while God's loyal followers — those who'd stood by him at Armageddon — offered open arms to the newly reborn souls. Rachel read on a bit — "Give it a chance," Avril had pleaded — and then, tired of prophecies and parables, their simple hope, she let the book fall shut.

Rachel stared at the bedroom ceiling as the old clock chimed and reminded her of days on the farm, the early hours of winter dawn when Harris would rise and chop kindling for the stove, set a fire blazing so she wouldn't have to get up to a cold kitchen. She admitted defeat. She pushed back the covers and got up. Although the house had cooled off — there had been a heavy frost — Rachel didn't allow herself to turn up the heat, only pulled on the heavy socks and a thick cardigan she kept at the end of her bed.

She wandered into the living room, found the light switch and winced, then headed for the kitchen. Out in the pantry, the cat was standing, shivering, swaying, almost tottering on its legs, a kind of grotesque puppet that bobbed in the weak glow of the night light. From under its tail flowed a thin stream of shit that puddled on the linoleum around its feet. She spoke to the cat, told it not to worry, that she would take care of everything. She grabbed a rag and filled a bowl with warm water to clean up the mess. The cat wandered in a halting circle. Its choked, strangled voice conveyed its terror. She coaxed the cat back onto the blanket. She turned up the heat. The cat hadn't touched the water, so she took a spoon and dribbled a little into its mouth.

*There's no sleeping now,* Rachel told herself and set about dragging into the kitchen the least cumbersome of the living room armchairs, along the way grabbing a blanket from the linen closet. She set the chair facing the open pantry door. Newspaper horrors long buried in her memory exhumed themselves, tales of cruel boys who used cigarettes and razor blades and worse to torment animals. "You escaped," she said to the cat, "and I nearly drove by."

Warm furnace air, the frost settling on the grass outside, the memory of those warehouse steam vents (probably cold now and waiting for dawn), the cat's steady breathing, all the feelings each of these things generated inside Rachel, the single facts of her day, began to cast a spell in the room, a soft cloud of comfort that put her at ease in her chair, started her thinking, prodded her into reflection. Rachel found herself wanting to say something. Not anything in particular. She just wanted to talk. The sound of a voice, even her voice, muted by night and by the canopy of nights she held over her heart, this was what she wanted to hear. She wanted to remind herself just why she was in this town, this house. Words hung in the air in front of her, whole sentences, and when she started speaking she addressed herself again to the cat.

She told the cat about Harris, about how she'd met him late in his life, a difficult, curmudgeonly, earthbound man who was not a farmer, who always told her he might never have been anything at all if he hadn't met her. At that time Rachel was a young and ambitious recruit to the small town's only firm of accountants. She gave it up the second Harris asked her to go away with him, to follow his gaunt and awkward frame, 18 years her senior, back into the hills and forests to his farm. If it was a lucky year, there were no cougars coming down from the hills, no drought, no disease, no flood. For three years she didn't get pregnant — three years of talk and more talk, the bull work of young marriage — but when she did she had no morning sickness, no miscarriage and no labour to speak of. Avril was born during a thunderstorm and had no flaws.

When things were bad, they had no market for their sheep, no luck with the weather, no feed and almost always no money. She could have put up with all of that, eyes closed, but in the end there was no time. Harris was out moving some irrigation pipes when the aneurysm, a balloon in his brain, finally burst. She had told him only that morning of a dream: he had retired and they had moved to Egypt to live in one of the pyramids. *Retired,* she had repeated, *just imagine!* His last words to her were "You got the tired part right, chum," and he walked off to the fields.

Avril was seven then, eight when Rachel sold the farm and made the big move to the city. Avril went to schools with 20 times the population she was used to and fewer friends. She grew smaller, scared; there were no tantrums but also no adolescence. She married early and found religion. *She wants a better world and I can't blame her,* Rachel thought.

In her armchair, the blanket tucked under her feet, Rachel felt as she used to feel in the bed she and Harris shared for ten years. "Cat," she said finally, "I miss him still."

The sun crested the neighbour's roof around 8:30 and entered the kitchen through yellow venetians, its light diffusing into a rich, warm rectangle of gold. Rachel had fallen asleep an hour or so before dawn. The comforting regular thrum of the furnace, the late night and now the drowsy sun served to carry her aloft, dreamless, well past the normal hour of her waking, which on this day was as easy and gentle as moving from one pool of warm water to another.

The cat was busy, its chin tucked under so that it could lick the fur on its neck. It sniffed at one of the burns on its foreleg, worried it a bit and then washed the fur around the wound. Rachel watched it at its work, marvelled at the animal's industry so soon after its ordeal. *An egg*, she thought, *with a bit of milk. Surely it can handle that.*

By the time she had fed both herself and the cat, it was well after nine. Out the kitchen window she saw a big Siamese pad across the back lawn.

"You need a name," she said to the cat, who was revisiting its breakfast. "Any animal with as much spunk as you have ought to have a good name. My brother was in the war and came back without a single scratch. His name was Timothy. I think that's a fine name."

Behind Rachel the sound of the doorbell echoed down the hall and she left the dishes to answer the door. It was Avril, standing on the other side of the screen door, both hands clutching the straps of her bag.

"Avril? Did I forget something?" she asked. Rachel worried about the looming spectre of senility, the tide of humiliation she knew would accompany its onset. "Are we supposed to be somewhere?" She made no move to open the screen door.

"You're not up?" Avril asked. "It's after nine. I thought for sure...."

"No. Come in, come in." Rachel pushed on the catch and released the door. "I slept late." She started back down the hall ahead of Avril. "Let me throw on the kettle. Do you want some coffee?"

"No, I've eaten already. I took the early bus." Avril went over and touched the armchair, still in the centre of the kitchen floor. She sat down in it as though she hadn't noticed the incongruity, her eyes distant. She raised her head and stared through the open pantry door. "Is that the cat?" Avril asked. "I thought you went to the SPCA."

"Well, I didn't," Rachel said. "He's a good cat. I've decided to call him Timothy. He's going to be fine."

Avril stood and stared at her mother. "Timothy? Uncle Timothy?"

"It's good, isn't it? Now help me move this chair. I had a hell of a time." Rachel nearly kicked herself.

They manoeuvred the heavily stuffed wingback along the hall and returned it to the living room, where they both stood awkwardly for a minute and examined the chair, its legs repositioned in the same indentations in the green wall-to-wall carpet. Avril removed her coat and looked around. She folded the coat and draped it over the arm of the sofa and sat down. She did not spread herself out. She did not lean back into the cushions or stretch her legs under the coffee table. Rather, she hovered, her head bowed slightly, as though she were trying to take up as little space as possible.

"I should have called," Avril said, "told you I was coming, I mean. But I didn't want to. I didn't want to phone. I just felt bad, I guess. About yesterday."

Rachel looked at her daughter, at the aching, submerged person she had become and realized that nothing could hurt more than the sight of one's own child diminished, paper-thin from years of worry and fear. "Don't be silly," Rachel said. "Yesterday was interesting. They were good people."

Avril pursed her lips and stared off to Rachel's left. "No, it wasn't right," she said, "to trick you, I mean. I should've just told you where we were going and let you decide. I was wrong. I was wrong to do that to you."

"Avril," Rachel said, "you did what you did because you care."

"I was selfish. I wanted us to…. "

"No," Rachel said quickly. "You have a big heart. I understand that. I was angry for a while, but I'm not angry now. I even looked at that book they gave me. I'll read it right through, I promise. Harris and I never talked about these things, that's all."

"You started reading it?" Avril asked.

"The chapter on the resurrection," Rachel said. "I read that one."

She saw her daughter look up, her eyes guarded, unsure. *How long has it been,* Rachel asked herself. *How long have I left you on your own?* She saw in her daughter's face all the years following Harris's death, wave after wave of days, and with them Avril, always Avril, like a mirror in which Rachel couldn't fail to see her own distraught reflection. Somewhere along the way she'd made herself believe that when she'd buried Harris she'd erased him from her life and she'd always assumed Avril had done the same.

"Look," Rachel said, "I'm going to get dressed and then I'm going to put on some coffee. I think we need some, don't you?" Rachel rose.

"Sure," Avril said. "Why not? I could use a cup now. But let me do it."

"All right," Rachel said, surprising herself. "You know where everything is."

# MAINTENANCE

"**W**ho are you?" Thomas said into the receiver of the worn, company-issue black wall phone. He shouted the words, not because the connection was bad, but because he had just come in from the backyard and had forgotten to remove the toque covering his ears.

"It's automatic," a voice said. "A computer does it. Your name came up and I phoned you."

"I can't hear," Thomas said.

"Can you confirm your address, please?"

"I'm hanging up now," Thomas said. "Goodbye."

Thomas returned to the back deck, sat down on the top step and placed a snarl of Christmas lights, lit up for inspection, in his lap. It was mid-December and grey. The reds and greens and blues he was studying were weak and ineffective, a bit ill looking. Several packets of unopened bulbs lay at his side. Behind him the neighbour's hedge hugged the ground against the weight of another wet winter and the planks and railings of Thomas's deck glistened, still slick with yesterday's snow.

"Christ almighty." His words fell into the damp air. For weeks now Thomas had been receiving notices from mutual fund companies, life insurance agents, funeral park operators, congratulating him on his upcoming 65th birthday and reminding him of the need to update his policies. He unscrewed a dead green bulb, discarded it and wrenched a red replacement from one of the packets he'd purchased at London Drugs. "On a Sunday too." A rosy light pulsed lamely in his left hand, painting his fingers a healthy pink one second, a stiff pale white the next.

The cat from two doors down followed a communal trail across the back of Thomas's property on its way to the next yard. Each of its paws hovered an instant before settling on the earth, a kind of unnecessary precision he sometimes saw at the Cock Pheasant waiting in line at the salad bar, hands threatening to light on a dish of chick peas and then drawing back.

"When do they leave you alone?" Thomas asked aloud. "Isn't it time people left me the hell alone?" Days just used to be days, Thomas thought. Now they're the days I have left.

When, finally, each bulb blinked or sparkled or pulsed, Thomas unplugged the bundle, scooped up the stepladder and walked down the driveway to the front yard. He saw the first flamingo as he rounded the corner of the house, the creature's plastic beak swaying slightly in the breeze as the body balanced on two metal spikes. More came into view with every step he took, until he could see his entire front yard populated by the pink ornaments. Each one had a red-and-white cap draped over its head and a dozen or so were pulling a cardboard sleigh that carried a sign: "Happy 65th!"

Thomas looked around. Where was the camera? Wasn't anyone going to jump out and shout "Surprise!"? He walked among the flamingos. Somebody must have left a clue. The kind of mind that thought of such a stunt wouldn't have the sense to remain invisible. He glanced up to see if anyone was watching him, but the sidewalk was empty and the street all but bare.

Nobody looked out from the neighbours' picture windows across from him. An anonymous joke, it seemed, the kind of prank Thomas associated with people who wore team jackets bearing crests and carefully stitched names such as Cindy or Luke. He decided the best thing was to ignore it. Any reaction, angry or otherwise, was more than it deserved. He worked his way across the lawn with the ladder and his string of lights. "Christmas," he said under his breath, "and now this."

Thomas had not intended to resurrect tradition — lights, a tree, the wreath on the door. He had not meant for this Christmas to be any different from last Christmas or the five others that had preceded it without fanfare, without celebration, without anything to mark the day as exceptional, no acknowledgement of the feverish activity of his neighbours, the local stores. It was a miracle any decorations remained in the house at all after the big garage sale two years ago. Only laziness and inaccessibility had prevented Thomas from lugging them out to the front yard with all the rest of the books, toys, antique kitchen gear that disappeared into the trunks of passing cars during the course of that day.

But a week ago his son, Keith, had phoned to tell him that he was coming west for the Christmas holidays and that it might be nice if Thomas could brighten up the place for the kids. He hadn't actually said the house was a mess, because it wasn't. It never had been. Thomas was thorough with the vacuum and never allowed dishes to accumulate. The yard was simple: a few beds of low-maintenance shrubs, a lawn out front and a small vegetable plot in the backyard, a "salad garden" Thomas's wife had called it. A very efficient home, but one that held no appeal for children. So, despite his initial impulse to say no, Thomas had allowed himself to be lectured a little on the need to stay close and on how children without a mother needed extra attention, a few surprises. After hanging up, Thomas had wondered whether it was his own urge to maintain a distance that had prompted Keith to call, as though he'd sensed his father's repulsion and was drawn to it the way a pet seeks out the one person in the room who dislikes animals.

The next morning it had taken Thomas nearly half an hour to pull box after box from the attic to uncover the mandarin orange crate that contained the tree ornaments and a few minutes later the lights, still in their original cartons. He had watched his feet climb the stairs to the bedroom storey, he had seen his hand open the latched wooden door that led into the unheated recesses of the roof, and, when the pull chain of the bare bulb had clicked the rafters and shingle strapping into bright, shadowy relief, he had understood again how attics had become a metaphor for the subconscious. Anything could pop out. If only there were a garage sale for all the garbage we carry around in our heads.

The other week Thomas had resurrected the evening he drove his son and a girlfriend to some rock 'n' roll movie about a band that broke up when one of its members died. Thomas couldn't remember if she was the girlfriend who later became his daughter-in-law and even later his ex-daughter-in-law. Maybe she was. He'd just bought a new car and the girl was admiring the lighted vanity mirror on the passenger side.

"That's not all," Thomas said, as he pulled down his own visor to show her a similar lighted mirror. "Now they put one in for vain men too."

The girl turned to him and stared. "What makes you think it's the man who does the driving?"

On his knees in the garden, at the stove, cracking eggs for an omelette, memories like this one came unbidden, scenes that more and more resembled a single thought, an idea he'd been carrying for the past 65 years, a large and sometimes troublesome notion that, despite his common sense, he had taken to calling his "life." Thomas had always maintained a strong distrust of people who talked about their "lives," who acted as if they were progressing through some coherent, orderly novel that contained a beginning, a middle and an end. He suspected them of narcissism, an understandable disease in an age when television and movies invited everyone to be a hero for an hour or two. Thomas himself had fallen into this trap at the local shopping plaza.

"How's things, Mr. Carson?" a clerk at the checkout had asked.

"Oh, let's see," he'd said. "I'm retired, I have no debts and my health is good. My life's working out just fine, wouldn't you say?"

"Sounds good to me," she'd said.

And probably it had sounded good. Just what she'd wanted to hear. But the incident continued to bother Thomas. It wouldn't have done any good to tell her the only reason he didn't kill himself was that exchanging one boring, senseless condition for another was what was wrong with the world in the first place. A gun was really just a different kind of remote control. Change the channel, please, I've seen this before. Nobody wanted to listen to that kind of talk from customers. Even Thomas didn't like to hear his own bleak thoughts, but of course he had no choice. Maybe the lure of a change was why he had agreed to host his son and grandchildren for the holidays. He told himself something must have tilted inside him, some weight shifted, a balance lost or achieved. Since his wife had died, he'd avoided the season like a ship avoids an iceberg, yet now here he was turning the wheel dead into it.

⌗

The front of Thomas's house had one long eave, well over 30 feet from end to end. Years ago, when Thomas and Katherine first moved in, before Keith was born, Thomas climbed up with the same ladder he was carrying now to attach a small brass hook to each rafter. He had wanted to show that Thomas Carson and his brood were of one mind about tinsel and holly and shortbread and eggnog. From December 1st until a week after New Year's, their street became Candy Cane Lane, every house transformed into Santa's Workshop ablaze with giant candles, winking elves, hundreds of reindeer. Every possible branch, wrought-iron railing, gable, chimney stack and bay window was decked with lights. The previous occupants of Thomas's house had been wholehearted supporters of the cause, so pressure from neighbours had compelled Thomas to continue the tradition, though his meagre efforts fell far short of the street's standards. Relations between Thomas and the Candy Cane crowd were cool at best, but when he ceased to participate altogether after Katherine died, complete silence descended. He had no idea how his return to the fold would be received, nor did he care.

Thomas' little brass hooks had turned black over the years and now there was an outdoor electrical plug, where before there had been a series of extension cords threaded through a window in the basement. Thomas positioned the stepladder at the far side of the roof after first displacing two flamingos that stood in his way. He would work his way across to the outdoor receptacle near the driveway, descending every third rafter to move the ladder. He had tried leaving the lights up all year once in an effort to avoid the tedious task of installation and removal, but the coloured paint on the bulbs faded and flaked after only one summer. Now he coiled the string of lights carefully on the ground so that it would unwind easily on demand as he moved from rafter to rafter.

The grass was sodden and he chided himself for wearing his walking shoes and not his work boots. Thomas hated them for the way they looked and for the number of people his age who had taken to wearing them, but it was better to be comfortable. In other ways, though, he had refused to keep up with the times. He'd declined to buy a computer when everyone was lining up for them, had cut off the cable the moment Katherine no longer knew what a television was, had insisted on keeping the rotary phone that had come with the house. He had a stack of CDs that had accumulated as presents over the years but no CD player. He still went to the Cock Pheasant, where a good meal cost no more than $7.50, coffee and dessert included.

Thomas looked up at the roof line and the bare limbs of the maple tree that he routinely hacked at with a pruning saw to deter leaves and seeds from falling into his gutters. Each butchered stump testified to the years he'd expended in maintaining this house: propping up its fences, clearing its drains and raking its lawns, scraping and painting its weathered siding. He shook his head. We come into this world to look after things and then we leave. It suddenly struck Thomas that for a while now he'd been seeing all his days with Katherine and Keith as photographs, black-and-white pictures, the small, crisp, wallet-sized kind his father used to take with a vintage Konica, pictures with their corners tucked into black triangular pockets, glossy and full of rich shadows.

"All aboard," Thomas said, one foot on the bottom of the ladder.

He climbed until he stood on the second-highest step, the tail end of the string of bulbs in his right hand. The eave was only a couple of feet above his head. Thomas reached up to use one of the protruding rafters to steady himself. He felt the eyes of the neighbourhood on him. Maybe his neighbours were telling themselves that a magical transformation was taking place. Old man Carson had had a revelation, a visitation, the ghost of Christmas past. After all these years, what could be possessing him? We thought he'd never get over the loss of his wife. Such a grump, but now look at him. Maybe the flamingos softened him up. Thomas could hear their maudlin, sterile thoughts. He could see their eyes brimming with flashy tears. What if he should slip and fall now? Crack a hip? Die? The irony would be unbearable.

Thomas shuddered. For 30 years he'd taught writing and literature to the great unwashed. Within a year of his retirement, Katherine wound down like the main spring of a clock, took to her bed and died. His students had always submitted stories with predictable endings, Thomas thought, and he had reprimanded them for it, but why, then, had he not seen this end coming, so predictable itself, and such a shock?

Only six days until Christmas. The air carried a hint of alpine frost in it, despite a salty wind and the occasional whiff of burning driftwood wafting into the quiet Sunday streets. Thomas draped the end of the electrical string over the first hook and pulled it until the plug at the end of the line jammed up against the brass fitting. So far, so good. He turned his attention to the next rafter, the one just above him, and then reached across to the third one. He used to do this with an audience, Keith and Katherine at the foot of the ladder warning him against reaching too far, placing their feet on the bottom rung, adding their weight to his.

"Don't be a hero," Katherine would say. "There are plenty of those in the cemetery already."

Each time he came down, she'd make a show of helping him move to the next spot, testing the ground before letting him ascend, keeping up a steady breeze of chatter and admonition as though her job was to ward off death by talking at it. Keith always grew bored after a while and went inside to watch from the living room window. After a few years, he just stayed inside.

It was nearly noon by the time Thomas had strung the last rafter. He lay the ladder on its side and plugged in the lights. A wash of colour bathed the flamingos and the house's contours in warmth. Thomas extinguished the show with a firm pull. He hung the ladder in the garden shed, retrieved the unused bulbs from the back deck and walked into the kitchen, first wiping his shoes on the mat. From the cupboard above the sink, he pulled out a bottle of dry South African sherry. "Merry Christmas, Thomas," he said. He poured a little into a wine glass, looked at it, then poured in a little more. He pulled a chair from the kitchen table, opened the back door and sat down. There was enough tobacco in his pouch for one decent bowlful. This was perhaps the only concession he made to Katherine's memory, though even now Thomas knew that his decision not to foul the house with pipe smoke had more to do with conditioning than with consideration for his deceased wife.

The day was no brighter now than it had been at nine o'clock. Thomas sucked on his pipe and sipped his sherry. The thing was, he concluded, we have to go on. Someone has to pay the bills. Someone has to trim the hedge. All these stupid little jobs still need to be done. The world didn't end when Katherine died; it insisted on dropping through his mailbox at the same time every day and knocking on his door to sell him chocolates or ask him for a donation to the Kidney Foundation. He'd been outraged to discover the real cataclysm was not that the world would end all at once but that it was ending one person at a time.

Hunger prodded Thomas from his brown study. Cooking was out of the question in his present mood. He corked his sherry, locked up the house and walked down the front steps to the sidewalk, pausing to look at the flamingos. No attempt had been made to keep them vertical. Some leaned at impossible angles, others had fallen over. The greeting had been poorly done too. Its black characters were peeling from the cloud-shaped piece of cardboard on which they had been painted. He turned and walked past the busy, festive lawns of his neighbours, all tinfoil and plastic in the dull winter light. This close to zero hour, many kept the juice flowing all day long, some with tapes blaring carols and choral music.

The Cock Pheasant was nearly empty. Thomas looked through its windows, each pane dusted with canned snow: only a few heads at the tables and booths within. He was about to turn up the path to the entrance when two postmen shoved by him as he stood deliberating.

"But a little rougher," one said. "More like cement."

"Nice," the other said.

Maybe not today, Thomas told himself. The sherry had gentled his views. He felt the need for more convivial company. He walked on to the corner, where a waft of boozy, smoke-laden air reached out to him through the open doors of the pub. Thomas stared past the foyer into the dimly lit interior. A shameless appeal to nostalgia, he thought: high English wainscoting, sepia photographs from the turn of the century,

Tiffany lamps. Katherine used to goad him into going there for a treat when Keith spent the night with a friend. They'd order a pint or two and share a salad and fries. Thomas hadn't stepped inside for years.

He found a table by the gas fire and looked over the menu. Pesto this, garlic that. Squid, roasted peppers, hummus. He settled on steamed mussels in butter and white wine with a side of bread, ordered a stout while he was waiting and watched a fight on the big-screen TV.

Keith's passion had been soccer and it had tried Thomas severely while it lasted, not because it occupied so much time with practices, tournaments and weekly games, but because Thomas was forced to care and with caring came disappointment and long, nail-biting minutes of anxiety, some of which became so unbearable that Thomas often left the field. Even the year Keith finally decided he no longer wanted to play, Thomas felt little relief. It was as though something had died and he mourned secretly for months. In the years that followed, during spring especially, he found himself moody and at loose ends when the big Saturday breakfast of pancakes and sausages wasn't followed by a search for cleats, jersey and shin pads and an ocean drive to the game.

The day Katherine hosted his retirement — Thomas was leaving the school's literary magazine, a journal he'd helped to start over 20 years earlier — students from past graduating years came to celebrate his editorship, some of whom he'd worked with long after they'd left school to become writers and journalists. Thomas was helping Katherine load the dishwasher when he paused to thank her for her efforts and to tell her how satisfying the whole afternoon had been. Katherine said nothing, but Keith, who had graduated a few years earlier himself, dropped a pile of paper plates into the garbage and said, "You've sure had a lot of fun with other people's kids." Then he turned and left the room.

Thomas was startled by the accusation. While he thought he'd devoted countless weekends to cheering his son on the field, Keith saw his father as a deadbeat, someone who cared more about work than family. Selflessness wasn't something you could fake where children were concerned. It would have been better not to have gone to the park at all if his heart wasn't really in it. Since that day Thomas had not even glanced at a soccer game.

Boxing was different. It pulled Thomas in immediately. Always one of the two men in the ring awakened a sympathy in him and for that reason — and because television was a hole he knew he was only too willing to leap into — he hadn't renewed his cable subscription after Katherine died. He finished his stout and signalled the waiter for another one, holding his glass in one hand and tipping it beneath an imaginary spout. The mussels came and he ate slowly, forgetting about his food temporarily while he concentrated on the match. The heavier boxer was beginning to show signs of fatigue, the bounce in his step now nothing more than a flat-footed shuffle.

"Mr. Carson?" said someone just to his left.

Thomas turned to see a woman, late 20s, early 30s, sitting at a table beside him with another woman.

"I'm sorry," he said. Thomas knew she must have been a student of his at one time. A week didn't go by when he wasn't pulled aside on the street, yelled at from a car, or served in a department store by somebody who'd attended one of his classes. But the ability to retrieve names at will had left him and he knew better than to hope it would come to him eventually. She must have been an early victim, judging by her hands, the lines on her forehead.

The woman turned to her friend. "Lou," she said. "This is my English teacher."

"Hi," Lou said.

Thomas nodded.

"This is the man. The one I told you about."

"Listen," Thomas said, "you'll have to forgive me. I don't remember you."

"Son of a bitch you don't."

Thomas pulled himself up straighter in his chair and reached for the glasses that he kept on a rope around his neck.

"Take a real good look," the woman said.

Thomas glanced frantically at the waiter and then turned his attention to the face opposite him. She was older than he'd thought at first. Forties, maybe. Lots of foundation, hair colour fading on top. She could be anybody. "It's a blank," he said. "I'm sorry." Had he failed her? Had he caught her cheating? God knows he'd looked down a few blouses in his time, but with some girls there was nowhere else to look.

"You gave me my greatest moment. That poor dead boy and the whole school listening. I told you how they clapped, didn't I, Lou?"

"You did, honey," Lou said.

The waiter dropped off another round for the women and Thomas didn't object to a refill. A student was beaten once, killed years ago by a gang. The school hosted a memorial for students and family. English teachers were required to undertake a unit in sensitivity training. Thomas remembered the school assembly, the rows and rows of children who listened reverently to music students playing "Blowing in the Wind," the parents of the boy who broke down at the lectern and had to be led off the stage.

"Dan?" Thomas said. "Danny Elkins?"

"Well, howdy," she said, deepening her voice to a mock baritone. She took his hand and shook it. "Except you can call me Danielle."

"Danielle," he said. This was the boy Thomas had urged on, published; he'd spent hours working on his poetry, cutting, revising, praising. Now Danny was Danielle. He apologized. He told her he hadn't suspected anything at the time, that all he ever cared about was the poem on the page, not where it came from.

"Didn't I tell you, Lou?" she said. "Doesn't he say the sweetest things?"

"Yes, he does," Lou said.

Danielle was an esthetician. She'd just opened a business in the village and the blue-rinse crowd were lining up to get in. She told Thomas he was good for a free facial any time. Just because he was old didn't mean he had to look it. Then Lou leaned over and touched Danielle on her elbow and the two got up to leave, but not before Danielle kissed Thomas goodbye on the top of his balding head.

"I've never written anything as good since," she said. "Quit while you're ahead is what they say, but who can do that?"

"It's a nice trick," Thomas said, "if you can manage it."

"Good to meet you, Mr. Carson," Lou said. "Let's go, Danny."

Thomas lingered over his stout a while. He poked at the few remaining mussels. A basketball game had replaced the fight and certain patrons had rearranged their chairs for a better view. Thomas paid the bill and started back along the road that led to his house. It was after four and the street lamps were flicking on ahead of him as he walked. When he came to his own street, the traffic thickened considerably as cars waited to enter the cul-de-sac for a tour of the lights. Children pressed their faces to windows and parents held babies higher in their laps so they could see out. This place is a hazard, Thomas thought. One of these idiots is going to rear-end someone and send a kid flying into a windshield.

Thomas walked up the sidewalk to his own house. Someone had plugged in his lights for him while he'd been down at the pub and had even dumped some cotton batting on the lawn and added a "North Pole" sign to the flamingos' sleigh. For a moment he was angry with the anonymous editor, but the indignation gave way to incredulity. Was he so frightening? Did his neighbours have to sneak around and spruce up the house in his absence because they couldn't bear to talk to him directly? What a sorry state of affairs. He opened the front door, hung up his coat and, leaving the room in darkness, lay down on the couch in the living room to watch the beams of light travel along his ceiling, various shades of red and green and blue blinking outside the window. Words from people passing by reached through the glass like birdsong, lulling him into sleep.

Thomas dreamed he was climbing the stepladder outside his house. The Christmas lights were heavy chains wrapped around his neck and the weight of them pulled him off balance. He fell into the bushes below. He must have broken something in the fall, because he couldn't move. Surely someone passing would see him and come to his assistance. But nobody came. It started to rain. Would he have to wait until his son arrived? That wasn't for another day. He might die before then. A cat came and sniffed at him. It curled up on his chest and went to sleep. Thomas began to suffocate under the cat's weight.

With an enormous effort, Thomas pulled himself upright to find himself on the sofa, sweating from fright, the doorbell ringing. The street was dark, the crowds had gone. He looked out, but it seemed as if a forest had sprung up in only a few hours. The air was thick with branches and moss. He groped his way to the front door, forgetting about the lights he might have turned on, and when he opened it Katherine pushed by him into the front hall.

"Oh, Katherine," he said. "I'm so glad to see you. I've missed you. I really have." He went to hug her, but she started up the stairs to the second floor.

"I want to see Keith," she said.

"He's coming home," Thomas said. "He's on his way. And he's bringing the boys."

"Those brats," she said and ran up the stairs.

Thomas followed her. He watched as she opened door after door. He knew she was angry and he wanted to tell her how sorry he was she had died. She turned to him finally and placed a hand on his stomach. She grabbed his sagging flesh as though she wanted to tear it from his bones. She pulled and pulled until Thomas screamed and woke again, the Christmas lights still blinking above him and his bladder about to burst.

Thomas dragged himself to his feet, the dream still twitching just out of reach. "Beer," he muttered. Sleep dogged his footsteps. He tried to rub the dream from his eyes, but mussels and beer were like a soporific, so he gave up and went to bed.

⌗

He woke to the phone. The bedside clock read 8:35. It was Keith.

"What do you think?" Keith asked.

"About what?"

"Haven't you been outside yet?"

"I just woke up."

"So, you haven't seen them?"

Christ, Thomas thought. The flamingos. "Yes, I have. They came yesterday."

"Shit," Keith said. "I told them today."

"So, that was you?"

"I thought you'd get a kick out of them. Happy Birthday."

"Thanks. No, really," Thomas said, "I thought it was the neighbours."

"You wish," Keith said. "Not this time."

"I put up the lights again too," Thomas said.

"The old place must look like a nut house."

"Yes, it does," Thomas said. "You're still coming, aren't you?"

"I'm calling you on my cell. We're in our seats and buckled up, but the flight attendant wanted me to hang up five minutes ago. They're lighting the fuse as we speak."

"Don't say that," Thomas said. "Don't even joke about it."

"Grandpa better catch us. Right, guys? What do you say?"

Thomas heard giggling and then nothing.

## Acknowledgements

**THE BERLIN WALL:** *Border Crossings*, Spring 1996; *The Journey Prize Anthology* 9

**YELLOW WITH BLACK HORNS:** *Grain*, Summer 1996

**FAST**: Second-prize winner, *Prairie Fire* Fiction Contest, 1998; *Love and Pomegranates: An Anthology of Short Fiction* (Sono Nis 2000)

**IN BED:** *Event*, Summer 1995

**RHYMES WITH USELESS:** Shortlisted for the Writers' Union Short Prose Contest, 1996; Shortlisted for the *prism international* Fiction Contest

**SOMETIMES NIGHT NEVER ENDS:** *Quarry*, Spring 1990

**THE NEW WORLD:** *Blood and Aphorisms*, Summer 1996

**MAINTENANCE:** *Event*, Fall 1999

**DEAD**: Second-prize winner, *The Fiddlehead* Fiction Contest, 1999

**PIG ON A SPIT:** *Grain*, Fall 1999

**THE DAY THE LAKE WENT DOWN:** Shortlisted for the Canadian Literary Awards (CBC/*Saturday Night*) 2000

I'd like to thank the Canada Council for the Arts, the British Columbia Arts Council, and the Saanich School District, without whose financial help this book would not have been possible. I would also like to thank Linda Svendsen for her advice during the initial stages of the manuscript, Will Harvey, and especially Patricia Young, who will always be my first and best reader. Finally, I would like to express my gratitude to my editor, Joy Gugeler, whose keen editorial instincts have been invaluable.